Boogiepop
at Dawn

STORY **Kouhei Kadono**   ART **Kouji Ogata**

…it was a long time ago. Honestly, I don't want to talk about it. I don't want to talk about what happened…

I met him in the hospital where I was staying.
He was a detective. A very strange man.
But...also a very good one.
I think he either knew the right thing to do...
...or, at least attempted to find out what the right thing was.

What I'm doing now has definitely
been influenced...inspired...
Everything I do gives me the feeling
I'm doing it for someone else.

Her? She was...I dunno.
Possessed by fear.
She thought nothing was worth fearing.
Or perhaps she wanted to erase all fear from the world...
I couldn't say.

Speaking of strange men, how about my dad?
What was he thinking?
He was an odd father—less of a guardian
and more of a best friend.
I can't quite forgive…his death.

Everything happened like a storm.
It ended as soon as it began.
There were assassins and monsters mixed
up in it, and even a shinigami.
I think he made his name up on the spot…

Boogiepop…

Boogiepop
at Dawn

Boogiepop
at Dawn

written by
Kouhei Kadono

illustrated by
Kouji Ogata

Seven Seas
LOS ANGELES

BOOGIEPOP AT DAWN
© 1999 Kouhei Kadono
First published in 1999 by Media Works Inc., Tokyo, Japan.
English translation rights arranged with ASCII MEDIA WORKS.

STAFF CREDITS

English Translation: Andrew Cunningham
English Adaptation: Patrick King
English Novel Design: Nicky Lim

Publisher: Seven Seas Entertainment

Visit us online at **www.gomanga.com**

ISBN: 978-1-934876-06-0

Printed in Canada

First printing: August, 2008

10 9 8 7 6 5 4 3 2 1

table of contents

SEVEN SEAS' COMMITMENT TO TRANSLATION AUTHENTICITY

Japanese Name Order

To ensure maximum authenticity in Seven Seas' translation of *Boogiepop at Dawn*, all character names have been kept in their original Japanese name order with family name first and given name second. For copyright reasons, creator names appear in standard English name order.

Honorifics

In addition to preserving the original Japanese name order, Seven Seas is committed to ensuring that honorifics—polite speech that indicates a person's status or relationship towards another individual—are retained within this book. Politeness is an integral facet of Japanese culture and we believe that maintaining honorifics in our translations helps bring out the same character nuances as seen in the original work.

The following are some of the more common honorifics you may come across while reading this and other books:

-san – The most common of all honorifics, it is an all-purpose suffix that can be used in any situation where politeness is expected. Generally seen as the equivalent to Mr., Miss, Ms., Mrs., etc.

-sama – This suffix is one level higher than "-san" and is used to confer great respect upon an individual.

-dono – Stemming from the word "tono," meaning "lord," "-dono" signifies an even higher level than "-sama," and confers the utmost respect.

-kun – This suffix is commonly used at the end of boys' names to express either familiarity or endearment. It can also be used when addressing someone younger than oneself or of a lower status.

-chan – Another common honorific. This suffix is mainly used to express endearment towards girls, but can also be used when referring to little boys or even pets. Couples are also known to use the term amongst each other to convey a sense of cuteness and intimacy.

Sempai – This title is used towards one's senior or "superior" in a particular group or organization. "Sempai" is most often used in a school setting, where underclassmen refer to upperclassmen as "sempai," though it is also commonly said by employees when addressing fellow employees who hold seniority in the workplace.

Kouhai – This is the exact opposite of "sempai," and is used to refer to underclassmen in school, junior employees at the workplace, etc.

Sensei – Literally meaning "one who has come before," this title is used for teachers, doctors, or masters of any profession or art.

Oniisan – This title literally means "big brother." First and foremost, it is used by younger siblings towards older male siblings. It can be used by itself or attached to a person's name as a suffix (-niisan). It is often used by a younger person toward an older person unrelated by blood, but as a sign of respect. Other forms include the informal "oniichan" and the more respectful "oniisama."

Oneesan – This title is the female equivalent of "Oniisan" and means "big sister." Other forms include the informal "oneechan" and the more respectful "oneesama."

CHAPTER 1
The Piper at the Gates of Dawn

Echoes was walking through town. His eyes were vacant, his hair was a mess, and his buttons were undone. He staggered along.

The sky was dark. It was colder than it had been all day. The air was clear, free of moisture. Dawn was approaching.

"…………"

Echoes moved his legs forward, as if powered by some external force, dazed. He had no idea where he was going. He just felt that walking was better than standing still.

The streets were quiet. Nothing moved except a gentle breeze, but it made no sound. Echoes' footsteps produced the only sound he could hear.

"…………"

Echoes stopped walking. He looked blankly around.

How long had he been here? He couldn't remember. This did not seem like where he should have been.

Nothing moved. No one was around.

There were countless fractures in the pavement. Rubble was piled everywhere. Most of the buildings were broken, collapsed, or ready to topple over.

It was a desolate landscape.

"............"

Yet there were no cries of sorrow. No mangled bodies. There were no people anywhere.

Instead, there were only ruined buildings as far as he could see.

Everywhere he went he found destruction. Not once did he find anything moving, hear any voices, or see any signs of life.

Even now, the only motion came from the pre-dawn air drifting past him.

"............"

Echoes began walking again. As he walked, he tried to remember. What was he doing here?

He should not exist. His body had turned to particles, dissolved into nothing. So why was he wandering aimlessly through these ruins?

"............"

On he walked.

He had wandered like this before, but back then he had had a purpose. And there had been a girl on the street who had reached out to him with her hand.

She was not here anymore.

Nobody was.

As he walked, the sky began to lighten. Dawn was coming.

"............"

He looked blankly up at the feeble light.

And then, from somewhere far away, he heard music. It was not a mechanical broadcast, but a thin whistle blown by someone nearby.

"............!"

Echoes ran in the direction of the sound.

He ran and ran, passing ruin after ruin, the sound growing steadily louder, clearer. There were no other sounds, and so the faint tune had carried a considerable distance.

At last Echoes reached what must once have been a very large structure, judging from the size of the mountain of rubble—the corpse of a building.

A black shadow sat on top of the mountain, whistling to itself. It wore a large hat shaped like a black pipe, and its body was wrapped in a black cloak. There was black lipstick on its pale face.

In profile, the face looked rather lonely.

"…ah," Echoes said. He wasn't sure if the person was male or female. "Who are you?"

The shadow turned toward Echoes. "I hope the whistling didn't bother you," it said, with mock innocence. The voice was like a boy's, and yet like a girl's.

"No, not at all," Echoes said, shaking his head. He decided to ask a different question. "What are you doing here?"

"I could ask the same. Who are you? Why are you here, in the world after destruction?"

"My name is Echoes," he said.

"Oh?" the cloaked figure said, pursing his lips. "So *you're* Echoes!"

"…you know me?" Echoes asked, surprised.

The stranger answered warmly, "You're friends with Kamikishiro Naoko, right? The person who came here from someplace else."

"I'm impressed," Echoes said. "That's exactly right."

The dark figure shrugged. "Kirima Nagi and Niitoki Kei told me about you. It seems we have a lot in common." Then it cocked its head. "I also heard about your mission. So, Echoes…tell me. In the end, which did you choose?"

Echoes just shook his head. "I don't know."

"Oh?"

"I…" Echoes began, then hesitated for a moment. "…I was unable to speak to people before. I believe I am only able to do so now because I am just a shadow. I'm only an echo of myself, lingering on. I'm not really the one who was called Echoes. Thus, I don't know what he decided. His decision is headed somewhere very far away, speeding away forever."

The cloaked figure nodded. "That makes sense. That explains why you are here, in this distortion. You were wandering the gaps of space, and you happened to synchronize with this one."

"Who are you?"

"My name is Boogiepop."

"You have a strange name."

"As do you. But yours is a good name, very poetic," Boogiepop said, winking.

Echoes looked gloomy. "The method by which I earned this name was not so pleasant."

"But not all your memories of that name are unpleasant, are they? There were people who called you by that name happily."

Echoes shook his head. "That was not me. Those happy memories belong to the real Echoes, long since gone. I am merely an echo of him. I have done nothing to earn the honor of being loved."

"I see…you don't have an easy time of it either, do you?" Boogiepop said, sympathetic.

"And you? How did you come to get your name?"

"Oh," Boogiepop said, with a strange, crooked, half-smiling, half-mocking expression. "That's a long story. Do you have time to hear it, Echoes-kun?"

Echoes smiled ruefully. "Time no longer has any meaning for me. I can listen to all the stories you have to tell."

"I see. Then let me begin by telling you about the scarecrow."

"The what?"

"The scarecrow. A straw man used to keep crows away…"

CHAPTER 2
The End is the Beginning is the End

1

Kuroda Shinpei. That was the name the composite human Scarecrow used publicly.

His duties were investigative. He was not investigating anyone in particular, however. He had merely been told to look for people who "hold a possibility that does not yet exist." A possibility no one, least of all the person in question, was aware of.

It was Scarecrow's job to find it.

"A train is approaching. Please wait behind the yellow line…a train is approaching…"

In the morning, Shinpei boarded a crowded train and headed to the office like a typical human.

He usually wore a long dark gray coat and matching hat, but he removed his hat while on the train. He looked like any ordinary salaryman. His most distinctive feature was the unfastened belt on his coat.

"Ah…" the suit next to him groaned sleepily.

Up all night?

There were lines under the man's eyes. Shinpei could tell the man suffered from a chronic lack of sleep. He also dosed himself with vitamin drinks before leaving the house every morning. Shinpei could divulge a lot from people's faces.

He's got an ulcer. Bowels're a mess. His only saving grace is that his liver's still working. But if he keeps living like this it won't be long before that goes out, too.

He was an ordinary man. Shinpei shifted his attention elsewhere.

He looked at each of the passengers in the same way, careful not to let them notice his scrutiny. One was a thirtysomething office lady who, despite her plain features, appeared to have several different sexual partners. Another was an elderly clerk who was probably embezzling funds or something equally illicit. He looked ready to keel over from the stress.

There were all kinds of people.

Shinpei took a different route to work every day. It took more time than simply taking the shortest route, but he didn't have to worry about being late.

Two more trains and a bus later, he arrived at the Kuroda Detective Agency. It was located in the corner of a building with extremely cheap rent.

"Oh, Kuroda-san. You're in the office today?" the building superintendent asked, grinning. This man was ordinary. He did not know who Shinpei really was.

"Yeah, just hoping someone hires me soon," Shinpei said, shrugging. "This recession's killing me."

"But there's always work for detectives."

"There are plenty of jobs—but not any that pay."

They chatted for a moment longer, and at last Shinpei was in his office.

There were two doors, one of which had no lock. It served as the entrance to a waiting room for clients who dropped in while he was out. The second was the door to his private office.

Unlocking this second door, he found a person waiting for him inside.

"Yo, Scarecrow," she said, waving her hand. She looked like a girl of about seventeen, dressed casually in jeans and a denim jacket.

However, this girl had entered a locked office without leaving any signs of entry, and until he was in the room he had not been able to detect her presence.

She was like Shinpei.

"Hello, Pigeon," he sighed, taking off his hat and coat.

"I've got work for you. They want you to check up on Teratsuki Kyoichiro."

"Again? This is the fifth time."

The girl called Pigeon shrugged. "Axis has their eye on him. He's too successful."

"Maybe he's just that good. I can't see why having a knack for economics should be interpreted as preparation for betrayal."

As they talked, Shinpei filled the kettle at the sink and placed it on the gas burner. It was much hotter than was strictly legal. The pot was boiling in no time.

"You rig that yourself? That could get you evicted," the girl said, eying the burner with a grin.

"I hate waiting for it to boil. It's the aesthetics of it," he said, quickly setting up some coffee to drip.

"I'll take a Mandarin."

"Do I look like I'm running a café, here? No requests," he said, making her a cup of coffee as well, and taking the two cups over to the reception table.

She joined him there, took a sip of coffee, and hummed appreciatively.

"Always look forward to this when I come here. Scarecrow, you could do this for a living."

"Everyone knows detectives are picky with their coffee. Part of my camouflage."

"Ha ha ha, how thorough."

"So? Details?"

Her expression became serious. "The Towa Organization has raised its observation status of Teratsuki Kyoichiro to Level A."

"Eliminate at any sign of suspicious activity? That *is* serious," Shinpei said, gravely.

"For the duration of this duty you can set aside your primary mission. Not like you've found any MPLS around here anyway."

"Doesn't the Towa Organization prefer it that way?"

"Yeah. Nothing wrong with not having enemies."

Even so, while he was busy someone else would probably take over his regular duties. Since that person was just another pawn, Shinpei would not be told who'd be covering for him.

"Makes you wonder why they're working so hard to find enemies within," he muttered.

"I don't like it any more than you do, but his company *is* getting much too big."

"I doubt *he* wanted it to expand so much, but the investors *insist* that profits must always be better than they were the year before."

"You're defending him? Go ahead—that's fine with me. But you aren't getting out of the job. No matter what."

Once the Towa Organization made a decision, they never changed their minds.

"I know. I won't let sympathy color my investigation or my reports."

"Look out for yourself, 'kay?" She took another sip of coffee. "It smells so good…"

"The sort of smell that makes you want to keep on living?"

"Exactly. We aren't human, and we couldn't live without the Towa Organization."

"…I know."

"We both have to do what we have to do—and we have to work together on this. Right? As friends."

"A Scarecrow and a Pigeon? Not the best couple," Shinpei chuckled.

"It's crows that can't stand scarecrows, not pigeons," the girl giggled.

The bell on the outer door rang.

"Come in! It's not locked," Shinpei said, standing up to greet his client.

A woman came in. She looked like a housewife in her late thirties, and she was very nervous. *Probably here to find out if her husband's cheating.*

"Uh, um," she stammered.

"Please, sit down," Shinpei said, motioning her to the sofa. There was no need to worry about the room's previous occupant: the girl had already vanished without a trace, along with the cup of coffee she'd been drinking.

They moved among ordinary people, always careful to reveal nothing of their true selves.

That was the world they lived in.

2

The Towa Organization was a group…no, they were too large to be called a group. They were a conglomerate that spanned the globe, monitoring and experimenting.

They performed research on evolution. The Organization was driven to divine the source of human intelligence, to figure out what would come next, and ultimately to control the process that would get mankind there. More accurately, they were focused on keeping as much of humanity as possible in whatever that next step was. They saw it as a fight for survival. For them, it was an ongoing battle to ensure mankind would win the inevitable evolutionary war.

Their primary tools in the struggle consisted of

a great number of composite humans. These soldiers were created by the most advanced genetic research humanity had to offer. The basis of the research was a mystery—top secret even among the members of the Towa Organization. Kuroda Shinpei privately wondered if the source was something that had already out-evolved mankind. Of course, he never voiced his suspicion to anyone. If it was known that he was curious about it, he would have been disposed of immediately.

But—and this was also Shinpei's private theory—if that source was not the future, but simply an individual mutation, a freak, then what the Towa Organization was participating in was a farce of epic proportions.

And that might be perfectly appropriate for us…

Shinpei was walking through town, wearing his hat and dark gray coat, as always. He almost looked like a priest in the outfit. Children would occasionally point at him as he walked by, but for the most part his clothes did not stand out much in a crowd. The look was ideal for lurking undetected in dark places.

He started by taking care of his detective work. It

wasn't hard. He went directly to the cheating husband, and said, "Your wife knows you're cheating. Are you going to stop?"

The man promised to break it off immediately.

Satisfied, Shinpei took several photographs as proof of the man's "innocence," faking the times, and wrote a report claiming he had uncovered no suspicious activity.

Affairs could be smoothed over when they weren't serious. He usually did the same thing if the woman was cheating. Unless, of course, his client had hired him to help win a divorce settlement.

When he'd wrapped up the case, he hung an "on vacation" sign on the door of his office and went to work.

Teratsuki Kyoichiro—even Shinpei did not know the man's real name.

However, he was one of the Towa Organization's terminals, and like Shinpei, he was probably inhuman. Kyoichiro's mission was to create an environment that would allow the Towa Organization to experiment with various methods of economic distribution.

He had been very successful, and his company, MCE, was one of the most powerful in the country.

That, naturally, put the Organization on their guard. He was *too* successful.

Ironic...

Using ordinary investigative techniques, Shinpei made his rounds, checking up on MCE's reputation.

"Eh? Investigation? Ha ha ha, that's a waste of time."

"Poke 'em all you like—you'll get nothing out of it."

"Can't think of a single doubt I might have about them..."

"Well, it's a one-man company. But as long as that *one man* is raking in the cash, who cares?"

"Yeah, any deal you make with them turns into gold. Everywhere else you get paid late, if at all..."

Everywhere he went, he heard nothing but positive comments.

There were no problems of any kind. The first instruction all Towa Organization terminals received was to avoid suspicious activity. Clearly Teratsuki Kyoichiro adhered to the command with diligence.

The closest thing to an issue he could find was that they were a little too high profile. The Towa Organization frowned upon any sort of attention—good or bad—but having a good name was hardly something to be concerned about. Fame is fleeting. It would only take a little information manipulation for everyone to forget about MCE.

He investigated further, but found nothing particularly notable. Yet Shinpei was beginning to be bothered by just how perfect his results were.

The sheer ingenuity of it was beginning to smell like something he ran across in his work as a detective—alibi construction.

This guy's too good to be true…

He could not shake the feeling that something was amiss.

He reviewed Kyoichiro's cash flow again. His eyes caught on a property investment he'd overlooked the first time.

It was a donation to a prefectural general hospital. Not too uncommon, really. Private enterprises often voluntarily helped out hospitals and medical organizations.

But was this done entirely to incur good will? It wasn't the most efficient way to provide aid to a public services organization. Compared with the flawless performance everywhere else, this seemed…*nice.*

He had no real reason to be suspicious, but even so, Shinpei decided to check the hospital out.

Thus, he was walking through the streets, covered in dark gray, heading for the hospital.

On the way he bought a bouquet of flowers, disguising himself as a visitor. He amused himself by making a whimsical bouquet of peonies, golden lace, and garden bride. Roses were too hard-boiled for him—he preferred to avoid them.

The hospital was large. The building was an octagonal prism, thirteen stories tall. It was a strange shape, but presumably chosen because of space limitations combined with a desire to fill the available volume as effectively as possible.

"Teratsuki-shi certainly has a penchant for strange buildings…" Shinpei muttered as he went in. Due to the large size of the complex, there were a number of security guards monitoring the grounds. However, the main hospital area was open to anyone.

He wandered around briefly, searching for nothing in particular.

The first floor lobby was filled with people waiting for their prescriptions to get filled. Cleaning staff were scrubbing the tile floor. Children cried for no reason in particular. Upstairs, patients were sleeping, but recovering women were laughing loudly with visitors, heedless of the suffering around them. Nurses rushed back and forth, always on their feet.

Nothing out of the ordinary.

Was I overthinking it? Maybe it was *just a friendly gesture…*

Still holding the flowers, he headed downwards. Glancing at the floor guide near the entrance, he noticed an arrow pointing into the building next to the word "Garden."

"……?"

Curious, he followed the arrow.

The center of the octagonal prism was hollowed out, and there was a garden in the middle. The beautiful patch of green came as a shock here in the heart of the city.

"Wow…" Shinpei said, impressed, as he stepped out into the garden.

He looked up and saw an array of mirrors designed to focus sunlight down into the center of the building.

"Fancy…did Teratsuki-shi do that?" he muttered, and began wandering aimlessly around, admiring the lush vegetation.

"Heh heh," he heard someone chuckle.

He glanced toward the sound and saw a girl of about thirteen sitting on a nearby bench. She was looking at him and laughing. Judging from her pajamas, she was a patient here.

"You're quite the passionate man," she said. Her manner of speech sounded strangely masculine.

"It's very impressive," Shinpei said, with no trace of embarrassment. Something about gardens put people at their ease.

"Let me guess. You came to visit someone, but they weren't here, right?" she said, suddenly.

"Eh?"

"You went upstairs, and then came back down, but you still have your flowers. I saw you up there from here," she explained.

He had been walking next to the windows, he realized. But he had not happened to look down.

"That's a very good observation. Yeah, that's basically what happened," he said.

"Liar," she replied, teeming with confidence.

"You're just pretending to visit. You're only here to snoop around."

"Am I? What makes you think that?"

"Visitors only go to one floor. If you were trying to find a room, you would've looked more confused." She spoke calmly. Having such a conversation with a stranger did not appear unusual for her.

A strange child. For some reason, he felt like she was a little witch.

Yet despite her blunt manner of speaking, Shinpei was not at all put off by her. "I don't know what else to say—you got me. I'm a detective. Here for work."

"A detective? You have a card?"

Shinpei sat down next to her, and handed one over. "Here."

"Hmm, I see. Kuroda-san."

"What's your name, little Holmes?"

"I'm Nagi. Kirima Nagi."

She used a masculine pronoun to refer to herself. It seemed to fit.

"Nagi-chan…strange name."

"My father was eccentric. He gave me that name so I would remain calm and unflappable no matter what the situation."

"I think I like that."

"I don't. Not when I get teachers at school who can't read it and call me Kaze."

"Ha ha ha! That's fantastic!" Shinpei laughed.

Nagi chuckled too. She looked down at his card again. "Kuroda-san, what exactly are you investigating here?"

"Can't tell you that. Trade secret."

"Nothing to do with me?"

"Aren't you self-important! I run a serious business, you know. I don't have time to harass junior high school girls."

"That sounds particularly impressive coming from someone who was just slacking off work to wander around muttering, 'How pretty' while staring at plants," she retorted, grinning.

"You've got me there." They both laughed, shoulders shaking.

For a while they gazed at the flowers in silence.

"It's easy to relax here," Nagi said, expansively.

"You sick or something? You don't look all that…" Halfway through the question, Shinpei trailed off, realizing that she might not want to talk about it.

But Nagi did not appear to mind. "Yeah, well. I'm here for a kind of pain, really. Been here six months already."

"Six months? Then school…?"

"Leave of absence," she shrugged.

"Huh…"

"They don't know what's causing it. My body just suddenly starts to hurt a lot. The doctors keep telling me the problem's in my mind, not my body."

The way she spoke was so straightforward he couldn't believe she was mentally unstable.

"Doesn't seem likely…"

"Well, my family background is worse than the symptoms. I wouldn't be surprised if they tried to blame the problem on *that*."

"Huh…" was all Shinpei could say. He didn't know how to react. But there was one thing that bothered him. "Your body hurts? Like…how much?"

"Indescribably," Nagi said, grinning. She seemed at ease with it, but that just drove home how bad it must be. "I've told the doctors, but they just keep comparing it to growing pains. Pain-killers don't do much."

"Growing pains…"

"Growing pains," she explained, "are a kind of nerve pain borne from the rapid changes in a child's body and activities during growth periods. There's no treatment for them, but they vanish eventually when the child stops growing."

This was exactly what Shinpei had imagined she meant, and it rattled him.

Could she be…?

He must have looked grim, because Nagi slapped him on the back. "Don't look so gloomy!"

"S-sorry," he said, meaning it.

She broke up laughing. "You're quite a character, Kuroda-san."

"Am I?"

"Most grownups would never dream of apologizing to a kid like that."

"Detectives take everyone seriously. Anyone can be a criminal," he joked.

"Even kids?"

"That's a very basic trick."

Nagi cackled, "Oh yeah? Guess that makes me your number one suspect."

"Nah. The beautiful mysterious girl is such a cliché no mystery writer would go near you."

"Beautiful? So you're flirting with me now?"

"Well…"

At this point their conversation was interrupted by a voice behind them. "Kirima-san, time to go back to your room." It was the voice of a young woman.

"That's Dr. Kisugi. Gotta go," Nagi said, standing up. "See you later, detective."

"Yeah. Hey, take the flowers?" he suggested, holding out the deranged bouquet of peonies, golden lace, and garden bride.

"No thanks. I never take anything I don't need…" she grinned, and continued, "is what I'd usually say, but why not?" Nagi took the flowers from him.

"Thanks," Shinpei said, smiling back.

"Say, detective…if you've got time, you should check me out. You might find something interesting," Nagi suggested.

"Will do," he said, and a young doctor, presumably Dr. Kisugi, came into sight.

"What are you doing? You aren't well!"

"I know!" Nagi said, winking at Shinpei. She left the garden with the doctor.

Shinpei waved, watching her go.

3

He ultimately reported that his investigation of Teratsuki Kyoichiro had uncovered nothing out of the ordinary. Nothing his clients would care about, at least. If he had been an ordinary detective the fact that Teratsuki Kyoichiro had a number of mistresses, each of whom had children, would have been noteworthy, but that wasn't news his clients would care about. Synthetic humans could not produce children, so they were definitely not his. With that in mind, his lovers were nothing but a front to maintain the illusion of his humanity.

And so he headed back to the hospital.

This time he did not wander, but went directly to a room—a private room. He could hear girls' cheerful voices through the door.

He knocked.

"Coming!" a girl said brightly, and the door opened.

"Hello," he said, bowing his head.

The girl who had opened the door was wearing what looked like a junior high school uniform, and she frowned at him. "Who are you?"

"The detective Kirima-san summoned," he said, politely.

Nagi called out from the bed, "It's okay, Naoko. I know him."

"Oh? Okay then." Naoko appeared to be a friend of Nagi's. She dropped her guard, and waved him in, smiling.

"Detective…you have results?" Nagi asked, grinning.

"You could say that. Never thought you'd be a billionaire," Shinpei said, shaking his head.

"What? Detective, you were investigating Nagi?" Naoko asked, fascinated.

Innocently, Shinpei said, "She told me to."

Kirima Nagi.

Nagi was the only daughter of the writer Kirima Seiichi, who had died unexpectedly four years earlier. She inherited the rights to all of his works, which, even after his death, were still selling millions of copies a year. Naturally, those rights came with their share of trouble.

"At first I thought you might be pretending to be sick, and hiding here, but it looks like you really *are* sick. Unfortunately."

"Why unfortunately?"

"There's no benefit to being sick, is there?"

"Exactly," Naoko said, earnestly. "No matter how rich she is, she's still sick. Get better soon! I don't want to wind up too far ahead of you."

Her words were said in jest, but there was genuine concern behind them. She was a good girl.

The three of them chatted for a while about nothing in particular. Eventually, it was time for Naoko to go.

"I'd better be off, Nagi."

"Me too," Shinpei said, rising from his seat on the bed.

But Nagi stopped him, "Stay a little longer, Detective."

"Oh?" he started to sit down again, but Naoko turned around, halfway out the door, and beckoned to him.

"Detective, if I could have a moment?"

He glanced at Nagi, and then followed her out. As soon as they were out of sight, Naoko went for him.

"Detective, are you on Nagi's side?"

He thought before answering. "…at the moment I am neither friend nor foe."

"Be a friend. Please. That girl's playing it strong, but I think she still misses her father." Her eyes were serious.

"…I'll see what I can do."

"Really? Promise?"

"Yeah, I'll try."

Naoko was not so easily convinced. She made him swear to cut his pinky off if he was lying.

When he came back in, Nagi was laughing. "So much for being hard-boiled."

Shinpei winced. "…you heard?" Then he smiled. "She's a good friend."

"I know. I'm lucky to have her," Nagi nodded. "Now, to business…have you made up a bill yet?"

Shinpei grimaced. "What are you talking about?"

"Don't play dumb. You got my agent fired for embezzling, didn't you?"

"I did nothing. I just asked a couple of questions, and he suddenly promised to quit."

"So how come a large sum of money—matching exactly what was missing—was transferred into my account?"

"No idea. Maybe one of Kirima Seiichi's books had an unexpected reprint," Shinpei said, sticking to his guns.

Nagi glared at him for a long moment, but then she sighed. "You're a great detective, Kuroda-san."

"You think? I don't mind the compliment, but I'm afraid it takes more than that to convince me," he protested.

Nagi ignored him, and asked pointedly, "Why did you do it, Kuroda-san?"

Shinpei looked serious but said nothing.

"I hate thinking about stuff this way, but were you trying to win me over?"

"What if I was? Tell me to scram, and you'll never see me again." He shrugged.

"…………" Nagi fell silent for a moment, then

seemed to make up her mind. "Kuroda-san…I don't understand."

"What?"

"What I should do. Even if I get better, what kind of person should I be?" Her tone was somewhat disconnected.

Shinpei matched it. "What do you want to be?"

"Maybe a writer? Like my dad? Meet a great guy and get married? Use all that money and start a business? I don't know. None of those sound right."

She was completely calm, speaking as though she were discussing the dissection of a frog. This girl was much too smart—she saw the deceit that lay behind the promise of each potential destiny.

But she had not yet been convinced that she had no future. She may have considered the possibility, but she had no intention of becoming the heroine of a cheap tragedy.

Even if she knew the truth, she would probably stay that way.

"I don't believe anyone manages to live a life that 'sounds right,'" Shinpei muttered.

"Not even detectives? You don't think your job is worth it?"

"Nah. Detective work's a dirty business."

He saw himself as an informant, forced to spy on people who should have been on his side.

"Really? I was thinking I might want to be a kind of detective…" she said, flopping back on her pillows. "Maybe I should reconsider. Kuroda-san, you ever want to be anything besides a detective?"

"Hmm…maybe something like…a superhero?"

Nagi snorted, "Please."

"No, really. I mean it. Detectives get tied down by all kinds of boring stuff, but superheroes get to solve crimes without dealing with any of that other crap. I wouldn't mind doing that."

He was half joking, but Nagi became oddly serious. "Hmm…" she said, nodding. Then she looked up again, eyes glittering. "You should go for it. You'd make a good one."

"But how?"

"I'll sponsor you. You decide the rest!"

"Woah," Shinpei grimaced.

"Think about it!" Nagi said, eyes gleaming, leaning toward him.

"You shouldn't say things like that so easily. People will take advantage of you."

"Screw it; I've never been too fond of my money anyway. If it was you doing it, I wouldn't mind being cheated out of every last yen," she said, looking him right in the eye. He was reminded again just how young she really was.

"Nah, I wouldn't…" he started to say, and then he noticed something was terribly wrong. Nagi's face had suddenly crumpled, and she collapsed onto the sheets.

"…unh!" she groaned.

Shinpei's eyes widened. This must be the pain she had mentioned.

"Oh no! I'll call a doctor…!"

He reached out for the call button next to the bed, but Nagi suddenly grabbed his hand.

He looked toward her with a start, and she was glaring directly into his eyes, grimacing in pain. Her voice strangled, she rasped, "*Really*…think about it. *Please*."

Shinpei could say nothing. He just pressed the call button.

The doctor came running. It was not Dr. Kisugi, but a male doctor. Several nurses came in as well, and Shinpei was driven out of the room.

Even in the hall he could hear her groaning in pain.

When he saw the desperation in Nagi's eyes, Shinpei had realized something. She knew instinctively that she would never be cured.

He opened his hand, the hand Nagi had grabbed a moment before. Smoke rose from his palm. It was burning.

Because Nagi had grabbed him.

There was no doubt about it now.

She *was* experiencing growing pains, but it was not any normal kind of growth. She was *evolving*. She was definitely one of the MPLS the Towa Organization was working so hard to find.

What's more, he knew her evolution was destroying her body. She was destined for failure, unable to survive the change. She was an evolutionary dead end. No matter what any of her doctors did, she had no future.

"…………"

He stared down at his burned hand.

I've done it at last.

He had finally fulfilled his mission. He had found an MPLS. It was a huge success for his primary function. Even if she was a broken sample, every MPLS was valuable, worth securing for the research potential.

She would be taken to a facility, subjected to countless tests, and after they had finished experimenting with her while she was alive, her lifeless corpse would be dissected.

I've done it. All this time spent disguised as a detective has finally paid off. All those shoes worn away investigating love affairs was not for nothing.

He should've felt the bliss of success earned after so many years of empty results. But why did he not feel happy?

"…ha." Suddenly, face twitching, he started to laugh. "Ha ha ha ha, ha ha, ha ha ha ha ha…"

It was a hollow laugh that shook the air in the hospital, causing the temperature to drop. A cold echo spread out around him.

4

Mo Murder received emergency orders.

Publicly he was an ordinary salaryman named Sasaki Masanori, but in truth, he did not work for any company. There were records that could prove his employment at a major food manufacturer, but those were fakes provided by the Towa Organization. His real career was in a different field.

He was an assassin.

Mo Murder was a simple combat-type synthetic human, and it was his job to dispose of anyone who might harm the Towa Organization.

This time the call came to his cell phone while he was walking the streets as always, pretending to be a normal businessman while actually searching for signs of an MPLS.

"Sasaki here."

"…D3 in progress. Accept order at NH33W," a voice said in lightning-fast Hungarian, and then hung up.

He quickly headed to the specified location, an ordinary coffee shop named Changlese.

A contact was disguised as a waitress there, and she gave him further information which he immediately proceeded to act upon.

"…name of Scarecrow, human name Kuroda Shinpei. Kill on sight for treacherous actions. Namely, an attack on facility RS22TTU…"

Why the hell did he do that?

"Destroyed the facility, reasons unknown…damage concentrated on drugs and equipment."

Was he trying to get some sort of medicine or related equipment? What's he going to do with them?

He checked over his target's combat abilities, made a few educated guesses at his mental state, analyzing the data as best he could. But his conclusions were inadequate, based on insufficient data, so he was forced to decide his best plan was to exercise extreme caution and attack at full strength.

From the data, he chose an escape route that seemed

likely. His plan was based more on his finely honed instincts as an assassin than the unreliable data.

Mo Murder pursued Scarecrow like a hound
dog.

"Mm?"

On her way back from the restroom, Kisugi
Makiko noticed the hospital window was half open.
She frowned.

She was on duty in the psychiatric ward that night.
She was a new doctor, having just completed her resi-
dency, and was often given the unpopular jobs.

"That's strange…" she muttered, closing the window. Burglary seemed unlikely. This was the seventh
floor. No thief would climb this far up.

Had someone simply forgotten to close it? That
certainly seemed to be the most probable scenario. She
turned and began to head back to her office.

Then she heard something clink.

She stiffened, and called out toward the sound,
"Is someone there?"

From a different direction she heard a loud

pounding, and someone swearing. Kisugi Makiko ran toward the noise.

The door to the room of one of the patients she was counseling, Kirima Nagi, was half open and still moving. Yet, there was no sign of anyone inside.

"Wh-what…?" she stepped hesitantly into the room.

The window here was also open. She looked outside, but saw nothing but darkness.

The patient was sound asleep. Nothing seemed out of the ordinary. Perhaps she was hot—both of her arms were outside of her blanket.

"Mm?"

There was a small bottle under the bed.

It was a medical ampule, with the seal broken. About half-full, the contents had been carefully measured into a syringe. But used ampules were usually disposed of immediately.

It was very strange for one to be lying around like this.

And she had never seen this particular ampule being used in this hospital. Not only this hospital—she had never seen anything shaped quite like it in med school or in her years as a resident, either…

"............"

She found herself reflecting on the contempt she received from the head doctors on account of her gender, on the sneers of the older nurses because she was new, because she hadn't graduated from a particularly prestigious school.

Before she knew it, she was lowering the ampule into her pocket, careful not to spill any of its contents.

A moment later a security guard came running—he must have heard her voice.

"Dr. Kisugi, something wrong?"

Careful not to let him see how fast her heart was beating, she said quietly, "No, it was nothing."

The half-filled ampule was carried away unseen in Kisugi Makiko's pocket, moving to a place unrelated to the present situation.

Damn it! Like an amateur!

Mo Murder ground his teeth.

Scarecrow was fleeing through the nighttime streets. If Mo Murder had not let himself be so overcome with surprise that he made a sound and attracted the attention of that woman doctor, he would have been finished long ago.

But the hospital room Scarecrow had probably chosen at random to hide inside…Mo Murder had recognized the name of the patient, and it had rattled him.

Kirima Nagi—that man's daughter. The daughter of Kirima Seiichi, the man he had killed four years earlier.

Of all the places for him to hide…

Scarecrow had only gone to the hospital to acquire nourishment. Mo Murder had seen him stealing glucose. He was also injured, so he must have been looking for pain killers, as well.

He had probably ducked into that room to inject himself without anyone noticing. But for that room's occupant to be one of the few people who could ever have slowed Mo Murder down…it was a staggering coincidence.

But it was *a coincidence. This has nothing to do with that man. My fate is not still tied to his!*

Mo Murder shook his head, desperately trying to stop himself from thinking about Kirima Nagi.

Scarecrow was fast, but he was wounded, and could not run forever.

Mo Murder cleared his head, and put aside his blunder, like an athlete trying to achieve a come-from-behind victory.

Quietly and unerringly, he pursued his target.

5

As Shinpei ran, he asked himself, "Why?" over and over.

The assassin's attacks were astonishingly precise and swift. They were over in an instant, the assassin gone before he even had a chance to fight back. His assailant wasn't trying to finish him off directly; instead, he was just picking away, gradually weakening him.

It was working. Shinpei was beginning to believe he would not make it out of this alive.

But questions were still spinning around inside. *Why did I do that?*

She was just a kid—he'd spent a couple of hours with her at most. Why would he go and throw his life away for her?

He had stolen a powerful drug called the "Evolution Medicine" from a Towa Organization facility. Then he had injected Nagi with it (his hands had been shaking, so first he had taken some pain-killers as a sedative).

The medicine would accelerate the evolution of any human, but in Nagi's case, since she had already started to evolve, it would act as a vaccine against the possibility lurking within her body. At least, in theory. If all went well, her body would become that of an ordinary human again, and she would avoid being killed as an incomplete possibility.

He had carefully chosen the amount to inject, but even so, it was very risky. It might have no effect, and its potential side effects could easily kill her instead of saving her. If that happened, all of this would be in vain.

He knew that. So why had he risked everything on a gamble that *might* save her?

Honestly, what was I thinking?

The assassin's attacks came persistently. Eventually Shinpei was so badly injured he could barely stay on his feet. He had lost a lot of blood, and his eyes would not focus.

The assassin jumped out of an alley and struck him hard on the head.

But Shinpei still wore his hat, under which he had hidden a metal plate. The assassin's knife was deflected, twisting his assailant's hand awkwardly.

"Ack!"

"Ha! Gotcha…!" Shinpei cried, attempting to flee, but there was nowhere to run.

He staggered around the back of a building, across the grass, and collapsed to the ground.

"……ah………"

All his strength left him.

He looked up at the sky. It was morning now, and the sky was clear and blue. He hadn't noticed the transition from night to day.

There were a lot of people behind him. He wondered where he was, and then heard a voice over a loud speaker:

"Mourners attending the Miyashita funeral, please come to the main hall."

He could just make out a tall pipe rising to the sky, with smoke coming out.

A crematorium…huh…the perfect place…

He wasn't getting up again. No force of will could make him move—his body was dying. It was surprising enough that he'd managed to run this far.

"Really? Promise?"
"You should go for it."

Girls' voices were in his head.

But at the same time there was something un-pleasant rising up inside him, an agonizing pain.

Oh God. Even with all this, I'm still not...

But his thought was interrupted as he noticed the black shadow standing in front of him.

His eyes were too weak to see anything clearly, but he could tell it was not the assassin. It was too small. *A child, perhaps?*

In his blurred vision it looked less like a person and more like a pipe rising out of the ground.

"What are you doing?" it asked.

The voice was clear but he could not tell if the shadow was a boy or a girl.

"Not a lot," he tried to say, but his lips would not move properly, his voice barely made a sound. It felt like he was talking in his mind.

But the shadow seemed to have no problems understanding him. "But...you're dying," it said.

"Apparently."

"You aren't scared?"

"…sure I am."

"Then…then why are you so calm?"

It seemed like the tone of the voice changed suddenly in mid-sentence. It became somewhat mechanical—automatic.

"I *am* scared, but…I'm also really angry, so I guess that stops me from thinking about dying."

"You're angry?"

"At how lame I am."

"…you refer to your clothes? A strange hat, a dark coat…why do you dress like that?"

"….nothing to do with my clothes. I'm a scarecrow, you see. I like black things, like crows."

"Hmm."

"And what are you? A *shinigami*? Wait a minute longer, I'm almost ready for you."

"*Shinigami*?"

"I'm a lot like you, you know. A scarecrow and a crow together are a very bad omen…" he tried to smile, but couldn't quite manage it.

"Why are you angry?" the shadow asked, its tone oddly mocking.

"…guess I can tell a *shinigami*. You see, I tried to save a girl. In exchange for my life."

"Isn't that a good thing?"

"Yeah, but now…at the last minute…I'm kind of wishing I hadn't bothered. I'm thinking I did something stupid, something I shouldn't have done."

He gritted his teeth. He could barely talk, but somehow he continued the conversation—partially thinking it, partially muttering it. "It would've been better to have done nothing rather than end up all pathetic and lame…and it's like a bad joke…I'm the one, I'm the one who blathered on about superheroes, so cocky. But I'm nothing like that…there's no excuse for it. She said I could be one, but…"

This was awful, incredibly awful.

"…………"

The shadow listened quietly.

He groaned, "I should be punished for this. Someone should pass judgment on me…but there's no time. I'm dying. It'll all be over soon. With me still stuck here, undecided…"

The shadow interrupted him. "You want me to judge you?"

"…eh?"

"If I do that, will you become the superhero you want to be?"

"…………"

"Would you wish for the regret in your mind to be cast aside? Would you want your mental state to once more be one she can be proud of? To return to the moment when your mind was a beautiful thing?"

The shadow's voice was emotionless. It was mysterious, unfathomable.

"…………"

For a long moment, he did not respond, but at last the conversation in his mind resumed.

"What are you?"

"You called me a *shinigami*."

"…you're probably just a delusion, an illusion you see and hear as you die. A fragile hope, like a bubble, that will pop and vanish in a moment…you're kind of a creepy one, too."

"You think I'm nothing more than some kind of…sinister *bubble*?"

"Yeah…funny, really. The last thing I see is a strange kind of bizarre…"

He tried smiling again, but failed, ending with a very asymmetrical expression.

"You…"

"Mm?"

"You haven't answered yet. Will you choose to be as you were?" the shadow asked.

"Heh."

Shinpei did not know how he planned to answer. He waited expectantly, wondering what response his heart would produce.

6

"He was here."

Mo Murder approached the thing lying in a heap, half hidden in the grass behind the crematorium.

Scarecrow was not moving, showing no reaction to his approach. He was well and truly dead.

Mo Murder had expected as much. He had known the loss of blood would have killed him by now.

He had calmly waited until he would be able to deal with the corpse away from watching eyes. He pulled some chemicals that would help dispose of the body out of his bag.

"Still," he muttered, looking down at Scarecrow's face in death.

He looked so proud, like there was not a trace of regret over what he had done. His face was pale and bloodless, but there was something that still shone within it.

"How did he manage to die looking like that?"

Like he'd led a life worth living.

Mo Murder grumbled the whole time he was disposing of Scarecrow's corpse.

"The End is the Beginning is the End" closed.

CHAPTER 3
Style

1

The office currently overseeing the copyrights to the works of Kirima Seiichi, eight years after his death, was in the corner of a low-rent building away from the main traffic of the city.

The office manager was an eighteen-year-old high school girl named Kirima Nagi, who visited two or three times a month to clean. She conducted all actual business by mail, so the office was mainly used for storage.

There were two doors. The first had no lock, so that guests could enter and wait comfortably. The second door served as the true entrance to the office.

"............"

Nagi silently unlocked the three different locks on the door.

Inside, she looked around to see if anyone was there, a habit acquired long ago. Of course, there was no one here.

As always, this made her sigh.

She glanced at the shelves of her father's works, which lined the walls, and headed for the kitchen.

She took out the kettle, filled it with water, and placed it on the burner. The former resident had illegally altered the burner, and it was extremely powerful. The water boiled in no time at all.

She used the boiling water to make a pot of tea. Judging from the stains on the floor, the former occupant had been a coffee drinker, but she preferred tea.

"Coffee is what American detectives drink," she murmured absently.

She was here to clean, but instead she sprawled on the sofa, drinking several cups of tea and staring absently at the ceiling.

In all likelihood, nobody had ever seen her acting this lazy. Everyone thought of her as frighteningly collected, and she had earned herself the nickname "Fire Witch." She deliberately lived up to the part.

But in this one place she was free to be an ordinary, listless, apathetic high school girl, doing nothing at all.

Every now and then she whispered, "Not yet…still not there…" as if there were someone in the room with her.

By the time she found the office, the previous tenant had already vanished. Everything inside had been hauled away.

She had quickly decided to rent the empty office, shortly after she'd turned fourteen. Ever since, she had come here to do nothing.

Absently, she picked one of Kirima Seiichi's books up off the table. *The Victor's Principle, The Victim's Future.*

"Unfortunately, genuine effort is never understood by others. It is only understood when you emerge victorious, but when you win, the beauty of the effort extended is subverted into something else entirely. The true fruits of effort lie only within that which is sacrificed."

It was hard to understand what he was trying to say, but then ambiguity was a distinct characteristic of her father's writings. Nagi was never quite sure why they sold so well.

"Ah-ahhh," she said, tossing the book aside. "All my efforts are in vain, Dad…"

Muttering, she stood up, washed the cup and pot, and put them away.

Then she left the office without ever getting around to cleaning. She headed toward the parking meter where her bike was parked, but suddenly she frowned, staring at the garbage area on the ground beneath her.

She saw the battered body of a dead crow lying next to the garbage. It was not a particularly unusual place for a crow to die, but she bent down and picked it up without the slightest hesitation. She turned it over in her hands, examining it.

"…………"

There was no trace of the carefree expression that had been on her face a short moment ago. Her eyes were again those of the Fire Witch.

She stuffed the dead crow into a plastic bag, tied it shut, and stowed it away in her handbag.

Then she pulled out a cell phone and dialed it quickly. It rang once, and someone answered, "This is Habara."

"It's me, Kentaro," she said, using a masculine pronoun.

"Oh! What? Something happening?" Habara Kentaro burbled happily on the other end of the line. He was a year younger than Nagi.

"You free?"

"Couldn't be freer! What do you need? I'm up for anything!" he yelped, excitedly.

Nagi managed a pained smile, "Right, then I've got a favor to ask. Check out the garbage piles around the west side of town and see if there's something there."

"Garbage piles…hmm, and what am I looking for?"

"Dead animals."

"Ick! Why?"

"I'm not forcing you to do anything."

"N-no, I'll do it! Sure! Dead…like what?"

"Anything. Just see if anything's there, no need to bring any samples back."

She did not bother to mention that she would do that.

"Ok. If I'm on the west side, will you be checking the east?"

"Yeah. Meet me at the usual place on the national road. In two hours."

"Sure. Oh, hey…"

"What?"

"When we're done, mind if I eat at your place?"

Nagi smiled her pained smile again. "Hitting on Aya?"

"O-of course not!" Kentaro stammered, flustered.

"Just kidding," Nagi said, amused. "I'll call her."

"Great, thanks."

She should be thanking him, she thought, but hung up without saying so.

Her smile vanished, and she glared at the garbage pile again. "So," she said, her eyes gleaming.

2

It had been nearly five years since Kirima Nagi began secretly helping people.

She started right after she had abruptly recovered from the illness that kept her in the hospital for six months. Exactly why she had recovered remained a mystery. All she knew was that her body was healthy once again, and there were several months to go before she could reenter school.

She honed her weakened body by training with an old friend of her father's, her guardian, Sakakibara Gen. He was a karate expert, and in no time her physical instincts were sharp as a blade.

Afterward, Gen had found himself in a spot of trouble. It was serious enough that he had to leave Japan. When he left her, Nagi felt like she might have been able to save him if she had tried.

That event, along with a few other things, started her on her current trajectory.

When she began only *he* knew what she was doing, but now she had friends like Suema Kazuko, Niitoki Kei, and Habara Kentaro, who'd gotten mixed up in something she'd dealt with and afterward pledged to help her out when she needed it.

Nagi was doing her level best to avoid putting any of them in danger. In the past she had lost a very good friend because of her choice to involve the person in her business. Habara Kentaro, in particular, was continually sniffing around after her, poking his nose into dangerous places. That was exactly why Nagi had begun asking for his help when she was fairly sure matters would not turn out to be too dangerous. Not that Kentaro's abilities weren't impressive—he'd taken care of one big incident all on his own.

Even so, Nagi was constantly reminding herself not to rely on him unless it was absolutely safe—or absolutely necessary.

"Welcome home!"

When Nagi and Kentaro had finished their investigations and returned to Nagi's home, her housemate Orihata Aya greeted them brightly.

"Hey, Aya-chan! Long time no see!" Kentaro called out.

Aya snorted, "Habara-san, you were just here last week."

"Oh? Was I?"

Both of them laughed.

"That smells good. What is it?" Nagi asked, pulling her boots off.

"Beef stew. I was making a lot anyway, so when I heard Habara-san was coming…it was kind of a relief, honestly."

"You're so nice," Kentaro said, nodding earnestly. Then he suddenly asked, "Oh, right—mind if I wash my hands?"

He was off down the hall before anyone answered. He'd been over often enough to know where the washroom was.

Nagi shook her head.

Aya stared blankly after him. "What's with that?"

"Probably touched a dead cat or something," Nagi said.

Aya's eyes widened, "O-oh…"

"More importantly, dinner's waiting, right? Sorry we were late…"

"Oh, no, not at all," Aya said, shaking her head and smiling.

Looking at Aya, Nagi marveled again at how much happier the girl seemed. When they first started living together she had been very stiff, but she had opened up considerably since then.

She had originally been friends with Nagi's stepbrother, Masaki. But a certain incident had left her alone in the world, and Nagi had taken her in. Nagi was only a minor, but she was also wealthy.

No sooner had the three of them sat down to eat than Kentaro, spoon still in his mouth, moaned, "You're getting even better, Aya-chan!"

"Thank you!" she said, beaming.

"He's right. Your training's paying off," Nagi agreed, once she'd tasted it.

Aya was attending a cooking school. It was pretty intense—designed specifically for would-be professionals. Aya had decided that the best way to plan for her future was to ensure her employability, so she had quit high school and enrolled there.

"But I'm afraid it does taste a little burnt. That's a problem for stew," Nagi said.

Kentaro sighed dramatically. "Harsh, isn't she?"

"No, I actually prefer to have people come right out and tell me if something is wrong. Helps me improve," Aya said, smiling.

"She keeps pushing you too, huh? Bet it would be a lot more fun to cook for Masaki," Kentaro teased.

Aya turned bright red. "N-no, I…"

"Shame he's been confined to the dorm as punishment for truancy. You never see him!"

"Oh, but I don't…"

"She calls him every day," Nagi interrupted.

"Oh, she does? Hee hee hee."

"Augh…" Aya moaned, softly.

"But you do miss him, right?" Kentaro said, insistently.

Aya didn't answer.

Instead, Nagi said calmly, "They're better off apart for the moment. Give them both some time to cool their heads."

"Maybe so. Oh, Nagi, what's going on with the Taniguchi house? With Masaki in the dorm and you in the apartment, is anyone living there? Masaki's parents are still abroad, right?"

"It's empty," Nagi said, simply.

Kentaro grimaced. "That's a shame. If his parents come back and find the place deserted they'll be shocked."

"Do you want to live there—look after it? You can take the rent out of your pay. You should end up getting about fifty thousand yen a month."

"You always were stingy," Kentaro sighed, then began plowing through his stew. "Mm, this is *so* good!"

"There's plenty more!" Aya said, and Kentaro quickly held out his empty bowl.

Despite her complaints, Nagi ate steadily as well.

She felt very much at home.

"…corpses at about a third of the locations…?" Nagi said, glancing over the notes Kentaro had taken. They were done eating and had moved to the living room.

"Like you said, a decent number. They'll probably be eaten by other animals by tomorrow, but…"

"So many different kinds, too…" Aya said, glancing over the data. "Crows, rats…"

"The garbage areas…the animals would only have been able to feed for an hour or two before the garbage was collected. It was collected this morning, but then why didn't they take the dead animals? Or were they placed there after the trash was picked up?"

"But what for?"

"Hmm…maybe it was just a prank?"

"But if you put dead crows and rats in a garbage pile, nobody would notice. Pranksters would go for something more obvious."

"Good point."

"…………"

Based on the notes, Nagi began breaking down the data.

"Find anything?"

"The only noteworthy fact so far is that there are no corpses in the larger collection areas," Nagi said.

"Ah!" Aya exclaimed. "You're right!"

"I didn't notice. Yeah, they were all in narrow

residential streets, nothing near big apartment complexes or office buildings," Kentaro shook his head, bitter that he'd overlooked the pattern.

"But what does it mean?"

"Hmm…" Kentaro thought hard. "Maybe they were poisoned? The poison could've been mixed into the garbage. Maybe it *was* some sort of sick prank…"

"But if it was poison, the bodies wouldn't be damaged. Instead, they would have thrown up, and you'd see evidence of that," Aya pointed out.

"Urp," Kentaro said. "M-maybe the rats got them afterward?"

"Rats would have taken the whole body somewhere safe before consuming it."

"Urp." Kentaro clutched his head. "When Nagi first called I didn't think this was a big deal, but…the more I look at it, the less sense it makes."

"…………" Nagi silently pored over the information.

"Nagi, what do your instincts say?" Kentaro asked.

Aya nodded, clearly wanting to know. Both of them stared at Nagi.

"The corpses were not taken away, probably because it was against regulations," Nagi said quietly.

"Regulations? What do you mean?"

"No, wait…you mean the garbage collector's contracts? Corpses don't count as garbage?"

"Oh, that makes sense," Aya nodded.

Kentaro did as well, continuing, "If you put out oversized garbage it just gets left there as well. Dead animals are probably the same. That explains why they aren't left in the big places as well. Those places would have different people collecting, and it would all get hauled away together."

Nagi agreed. "Some of the garbage men probably picked it up without thinking. But if they left it there, they weren't being lazy. There are strict regulations about that sort of thing."

"So corpses weren't at a third of the places, but at a lot more?"

"It seems to be a reasonable assumption."

"Then what *is* going on? This is happening on such a large scale…" Kentaro groaned. "That makes me understand it even less!"

"…………"

Nagi stared down at the information without answering.

At two o'clock in the morning, Aya's eyes snapped open. The sound of the air conditioner through the wall had woken her.

She pulled a cardigan over her pajamas and left her room. Nagi was still up, with thin rubber gloves on, examining the dead crow on the table.

"Um," she said.

"You have school tomorrow," Nagi said, not turning around. "Go back to bed."

"Y-yeah…you too."

"Yeah. Just as soon as I check this one thing," she said, her hands never pausing. She would be up all night. She always was. She usually slept in class, instead.

"…………"

Aya stared at her back for a while.

After a minute, Nagi turned around. "What? Something on your mind?"

"N-not really. I just…you're really working hard, I thought."

"It's a habit by this point," Nagi said, shrugging.

"How do you do it?" Aya found herself asking.

"How? Hmm…let's see. Aya, why do you like Masaki?"

"Eh?" Aya said, surprised. "Uh, well, b-because…um…" She couldn't find the words.

Nagi grinned at her. "See? Not everything can be explained."

Aya was flustered now. She had only wanted to express her admiration. "…sorry," she said, lowering her gaze.

"Nothing to apologize for," Nagi grimaced, and turned back to her work.

Aya watched her a little longer.

Eventually, Nagi asked, "Aya, would you make some tea?"

"S-sure!" Aya said, brightening visibly. She bolted for the kitchen. "Earl Grey?"

"Yeah. In a pot. Milk on the side, I'll add it myself."

"Okay!" Aya said, happily.

Nagi smiled to herself. It was like they were newlyweds, she thought. *Or…or she's the adorable assistant of a worn-out detective…*

The role she'd never managed to adequately play. Nagi sighed, covered the dead crow with a sheet, and stood up.

3

"Nagi, what do you think being normal means?" Kirima Seiichi asked as he died. He was coughing up blood on the floor of his work room, gasping his last breath.

Nagi had said, "I-I'll call a doctor!" and tried to run off, but Seiichi just grabbed her hand and squeezed tightly.

Then he said, "Being normal means abandoning change…staying exactly the same forever. So if you don't want that…then you have to be something that isn't normal. That's why…why I…"

He was muttering words that made no sense. Nagi had already realized that he could not be saved.

She also was aware that he knew he was dying, as well.

Her father had something he could not tell her, but was trying to get something across anyway, which was why he was talking like that—she knew this instinctively.

But even so, Nagi could not answer Seiichi.

The ambulance arrived, and he was placed on a stretcher, but by then he was already dead. The cause of death was gastric perforation leading to dissolution of the internal organs. Everything around his stomach had melted.

People gossiped that he had worked himself to death. It was like he had died in battle, and his death seemed only to increase his popularity.

Nagi herself received a number of offers from the media. She bore a heavy burden, as she was the daughter of a celebrity and was also very beautiful.

But Nagi rejected every proposal. Some of them were very persistent, but Sakakibara Gen was able to help get rid of them.

Nagi occasionally asked Gen about her father's death.

"Sensei, did my father like his work?"

"Dunno."

Gen was a tall, skinny man with an impish expression. At a glance, you would never guess he was a martial artist. No matter what, his first reaction was to insist he knew nothing. It was hard to tell if he wanted her to think for herself or was just being cautious, but that's the kind of man he was.

"He always seemed like there was something driving him forward. Looking at it now, it's easy to say it was 'death,' but somehow I just can't quite make myself believe that."

He scratched his scraggly beard. "Then what was it?"

"Hmm. I just think he was pissed off. I mean, it was like he felt, 'Things ought to be working out okay, so why had the world turned out this way?' After all, he was an enemy of society."

That had been Kirima Seiichi's self-selected nickname.

"Pissed off…that's so simple it actually makes it harder to understand."

"Ha ha ha. Seiichi said that to me all the time. 'Gen, everything you say hits the truth with such accuracy it completely misses the point.'"

"But he was friendly with you. He didn't spend all his time being angry."

"No, well…he was never much good at meeting people, and would never work particularly hard at getting along with anyone."

"…yeah, like Mom?"

"…mmm, it's complicated," Gen sighed.

For a moment they sat in silence. Nagi was the first to break it. "Sensei," she said.

"What?"

"Did my father think he knew everything? That he was the smartest person in the world and could understand anything? Did he ever feel like that?"

"Not sure. Certainly he was smarter than anyone else I've ever met…but he always insisted that I was much smarter than him. 'Course, he might have just been making fun of me. But when he learned something he didn't know, he would always say, 'Fascinating.' He was never embarrassed by a lack of knowledge. And he often said that he was really an idiot, didn't he?"

"I never knew if he really meant that."

"Neither did I."

…even eight years later, Nagi never knew how serious her father had been.

It was early in the morning, just after dawn.

There was no one on the road running along the river. The only sound was the gentle burbling of the river water. There were homes nearby, but everyone was still sleeping. The area was one small gap in the constant bustle of the world.

They had recently finished repaving the road, and the new asphalt gleamed on the surface. Footsteps were tapping along it.

They came from a man in a suit and tie. He appeared to be a dedicated worker, a middle-aged government employee. There was a plastic garbage bag in his hand.

The dark shadow of exhaustion was on his face. He must have been under a lot of stress.

He sighed loudly, and hefted the garbage bag, staring at it contemplatively.

"Guess I should hurry," he said, and tossed it onto the garbage area next to the road. It was still early, and there were only two or three other bags there—probably put there the night before in defiance of regulations.

The man turned around, and headed back the way he had come.

"_____!"

He stopped a few seconds later. There was someone in front of him. *How long had she been there?*

"…I see. So it was you?"

The man went stiff. Not only because he'd been addressed directly, but also because this person was majestic, and seemed to be radiating a beautiful light.

She wore a leather jumpsuit and sturdy steel-tipped boots. It was Kirima Nagi.

The girl people called the Fire Witch.

"Wh-who are you?"

"Who I am is not important. The problem lies with you."

"Wh-what do you mean?"

"You're the bad guy, aren't you?" she said, abruptly.

The man gaped, taking a step backwards.

Nagi took a step forward. "I understand two things," Nagi explained. "First, that you were acting alone. This was not carried out by any group. Those clothes—that suit—is a fraud. Even if someone sees you, they'll just think you're a salaryman who's been asked to take out the trash. It keeps you from attracting suspicion. If you had help, you'd never need to do that—you could all coordinate your tasks together. This case had that air about it from the beginning, but now I'm sure of it."

The man flinched. She was unrelenting. But he quickly coughed and tried to gain the upper hand. "Who do you think you are? You look like you're still in high school! What are you blabbering on about, anyway? What case? What do you mean? I have no idea what this is about."

He seemed sure that children would be cowed if he just acted arrogant enough.

"What school do you go to? Depending on what you think you're doing, I may have to report this to your teachers!"

Certainly, the average high school student *would* get flustered if an adult suddenly scolded them. But Nagi was no ordinary girl.

She carried on as if he'd never spoken. "Second, you are acting calmly, in full knowledge of the possible consequences. That's why the hand that darted into your pocket when I called out to you swiftly came out empty. If you used the gun you're carrying you would not be able to talk your way out of this."

She pointed at the bulge in his pocket.

"............!" The man went pale.

"But judging from the size of that gun, it won't be very accurate. And the tension I'm sensing from you does not suggest you've used it a lot. At this distance you'll never hit me."

Nagi had been carefully maintaining the distance between them.

The man groaned, but tried again, "S-so what are you saying? What 'case' are you talking about?!"

"The dead crows," Nagi said, bluntly.

"Wh-what do those have to do…"

"The crows that died *attacking each other*."

The air shifted. The awkwardness vanished, replaced with a murderous tension.

"............"

The man was no longer putting on his act. His hand went into his pocket, and he pulled out the gun and pointed it at Nagi.

But he did not pull the trigger—he only held it steady. He asked, "How much do you know?"

"I'm absolutely sure you've been planting drugs disguised as garbage for the crows to eat. Everything beyond that is only supposition."

The gun did not waver, his eyebrows did not flicker.

"Tell me," the man hissed.

"I first thought something was strange when I noticed beak marks on the crows' bodies. The only explanation I could come up with is that they were attacking each other. Groups of crows have some unusual habits, one of which is to execute one of their members that has grown ill and begun exhibiting unusual behavior. But they would never do that where other animals would come to feed. They normally carry out such behavior somewhere safer, in seclusion from observers. But the dead crows had beak and claw marks on their bodies, and bits of what appeared to be crow flesh inside their own beaks. Which means, I surmised, they went unexpectedly berserk and attacked the other crows, which subsequently fought back. Why did that happen? You know better than I do."

"............"

"In my autopsy, I found traces of a food additive

that had an element that can only be described as a stimulant. But it was only a small amount, so something must have strengthened it…"

"Exactly!" the man yelled. "I am not scattering poison! The poison was already in the garbage!"

"And you drove the crows and rats in town to crazed violence to let people know that?" Nagi asked quietly.

The man glared at her.

Yes—that's what this case boiled down to. This oddly calculated plan had been lurking behind what appeared to be simply a dead crow in a garbage area.

"I did! How many crows and rats are there in the city? Millions! If they all turn violent at once, attacking people, everyone will assume it must be something in the food!"

The man shook, his voice tight with emotion.

"And when it turns out people are eating the same thing…"

There was grief in his eyes. Nagi knew what that grief meant. Those were the eyes of someone who had suffered a great loss.

"…childhood allergies?"

This man had most likely lost a child.

"…and nobody knows! That's why I had to make them understand! That's why…"

"In that case, you're finished," Nagi interrupted.

"Mm?" The man blinked at her. "What do you mean?"

"I *noticed*. You were doing this because nobody knew. But now that I've noticed the truth behind your actions, there's no need for you to continue."

She looked him right in the eye.

"…………"

The man was stunned.

She walked slowly toward him.

He watched her, dazed. He only recovered and tried to shake her off when she put her hand on the gun. A moment later his body was airborne, and he landed hard on his back.

Nagi's hand had twisted ever so slightly, but with enough force to send a grown man flying. It wasn't karate—this was an Aikido move.

"Hmm," she looked down at the gun, swiftly ejected the bullets, and then dropped it on the ground next to the man.

He'd hit his spine and could not stand up.

"Unh…!" he groaned, tears flowing down his cheeks.

Nagi addressed him coldly, "Think about it. If all the crows go berserk, they will attack the weak. Those in the greatest danger will be babies. Is that what you want?"

"Aauuuughh!" the man wailed, sobbing in earnest. All the tension had left him. "I just…I just…"

Ignoring him, she went over to the garbage bag and cut it open with a knife. It was filled with thinly sliced meat, with bits of paper and something white scattered over it. The "feed."

Nagi gathered that up and stuffed it in her bag, then closed the garbage bag again and put it back on the pile.

"So," she said, turning to leave.

"W-wait!" the man called out. He was on his feet—unsteady, but upright. "Why don't you arrest me?"

"You have not committed any crimes. No point in taking you to the police. The feed itself is probably not poisonous. Throwing it out in the garbage is not a crime unless I can prove cause and effect."

"B-but…!"

"Yeah. You're right. There is one person who thinks this is a crime. *You*. Even though you must have been the first to realize that crimes required proof."

"…………!"

"If you still have the resolve to tell the world, then do so. You are the only one who can." She turned her back on him again.

"…………"

The man hung his head, but a moment later looked up, and asked, "What is your name?"

Nagi did not turn around. "Unlike some people, I do not like giving out my name," she said, and walked away.

4

"So what was it all about?" Kentaro asked when Nagi came back to the bike where she'd left him waiting. "I basically get that this was all revenge for a baby that died when that guy fed it something with that additive in it, but why didn't he just take it to court in the first place?"

"He was probably too sad."

"Huh?"

"He most likely didn't think about *anything* for a year. Only afterward did he start to suspect that the additive might have been the cause of the tragedy. But after that much time had passed, it would be pretty hard to get anyone to listen to him. He was too late. And the manufacturer has really good lawyers."

"I see. So that's why he tried this…but should we really just let him go? Won't he go public with what he did?"

"He might."

"And he might tell everyone about you."

"I'm not so sure. I've decided I'm just going to take that risk," Nagi said, not sounding the least bit worried.

Kentaro stared at her for a moment, but eventually he sighed. "But if he goes public there will be all kinds of panic. Like all the fuss over Teratsuki Kyoichiro, or…or those serial killings five years ago, where that Sasaki Masanori guy almost killed Suema-san."

"…………"

Nagi grimaced. When he saw that, Kentaro sighed again.

The Sasaki Masanori incident had involved an ordinary food manufacturing company salaryman named Sasaki Masanori, who turned out to be a serial killer who had brutally murdered several young girls. Nagi's friend Suema Kazuko, who Kentaro had met several times now, had been on the killer's list and narrowly avoided becoming a victim.

According to the police reports, Sasaki Masanori

had been found hanging from a rope; a suicide.

But from what Suema had told him, the case had actually been solved in secret by Nagi herself, when she was only fourteen.

But whenever the subject came up, Nagi became obviously annoyed and refused to talk about it.

Kentaro felt hurt by this, frustrated that Nagi wouldn't open up to him, wouldn't trust him.

"Maybe you'd be better off if he *did* tell everyone. I mean, Nagi, you don't get any thanks for what you do."

Nagi grinned at him. "And who was it who snuck out the back door after wrapping up the Teratsuki Kyoichiro affair?"

She put her helmet on, threw her leg over her motorcycle, and started the engine.

"Yeah, well," Kentaro said, shrugging. "That's your style, isn't it?"

He was here on an ordinary bicycle. He put his helmet on, too.

They had plenty of time before school started, so

they took a leisurely ride down the river. The morning breeze was refreshing.

I might just stick to Nagi because I like moments like this... Kentaro grinned, riding alongside Nagi.

Suddenly, Nagi hit the brakes, stopping her motorcycle.

Kentaro pulled up as well, almost toppling over, but catching his balance at the last second.

"Wh-what?! Something wrong?!" Kentaro asked, but Nagi did not answer.

Her neck was bent, staring up at a building across the road. It was a strangely shaped—an octagonal prism. Pretty big, too.

"That's…"

"Yeah, one of the infamous Teratsuki-shi's eccentric buildings. It was a general hospital. Can't recall if it was prefectural or city, though," Kentaro said, pushing his bike back in her direction.

"It's…still there?" Nagi murmured.

"Yeah. It closed some time ago, but…all the properties he was involved with have proved really hard to dispose of. It must be slated for demolition soon. The creditors must own it by now."

"…………"

Nagi stared up at it a moment longer, and then abruptly wheeled her motorcycle around and sped off toward the structure.

Kentaro was baffled by her behavior, but followed her anyway.

The building was surrounded by chain link fences, with "No Trespassing" signs, but Nagi went right on in, and Kentaro followed, shaking his head.

"Ew, what a dump…" he said, as he stepped inside.

The interior was heavily deteriorated. Bed frames were piled high in the lobby, dust balls heaped on them like fluffy stuffed animals. The tiles on the floor were no longer attached, and shifted underfoot. Kentaro felt like he was walking on dead insects.

"Yuck. Nagi, what the hell are we doing here?"

Nagi ignored him, walking straight ahead. Judging from her lack of hesitation, she knew this place pretty well.

Oh! Maybe…

He'd heard Nagi had been sick in junior high, and spent a long time in the hospital. Maybe this was her hospital.

Lots of memories, then?

Nagi stepped out into the open space in the center of the building.

Kentaro heard her gasp, and poked his head out the door.

"Ah!" he yelped.

There was a shock of green. It was mostly weeds, but the leaves were lush, the white and yellow flowers bright, and he felt like they had stepped into a tropical paradise.

"Wow," Kentaro said, moving out into the garden and looking up.

It was open all the way to the top, and there were mirrors placed along the walls, reflecting light down to the bottom.

"…I see. This building's most eccentric feature. Drab on the outside, green on the inside…"

Of course, this had once been a proper, well-maintained garden. The trees must have been hauled away when the hospital closed. But the environment remained, and the garden had stayed alive.

"Amazing, isn't it, Nagi…?" Kentaro said, turning toward her, and trailing off mid-thought.

Nagi was crying. Her eyes were wide and her lips trembling, staring at the garden as tears flowed.

"'It's very impressive,'" she whispered, as if quoting someone else.

Kentaro was stunned. He could only stand and stare.

Nagi walked unsteadily away, and sat down on an overgrown bench. She hung her head, muttering to herself.

She seemed oddly childish, and Kentaro was starting to get worried. "Um," he said, hesitantly.

"What do you want to be?" Nagi suddenly asked.

"Eh?"

"In the future, what do you want to be?" she asked, not looking up.

"Wh-where'd that come from?"

"What do you think will become of me? What do you think I should be?" she muttered, emotionless.

"What will…aren't you already a hero?"

"Can I really? Can I really be one?"

"Well, you already…"

"'You should go for it,' I said. How thoughtless of me." Nagi smiled faintly, and fell silent.

Her shoulders looked so thin, so frail that Kentaro was suddenly reminded that the Fire Witch was just a high school girl.

"…I don't really know," Kentaro said, hesitantly. "But I think if anyone can do it, you can. I'm sure you will. And because I think that, I'm trying to…"

Help, he almost said, but suddenly hesitated. He was suddenly not sure that what he was doing was useful to her. It was fully possible he was just getting in her way, dragging her back.

"So, um…"

"…………"

Kentaro stood helplessly in front of Nagi. She said nothing for a long time, and then abruptly, "Think about it," she said.

"Think about whether I can be one."

"…………" Kentaro didn't even think it worth thinking about, but she seemed so earnest that he said, "…okay, I will."

Nagi reached up and wiped away her tears. When she looked up she was herself again.

"Thanks," she said, awkwardly.

Above their heads, the mirrors glittered, reflecting the light of the rising sun.

"Style" closed.

CHAPTER 4
God Only Knows

The sun reflected in the mirrors that lined the sides of the open central column of the hospital, glittering.

"...mm," Kisugi Makiko squinted at the sudden glare, walking down the fourth floor hallway.

She was a young doctor, only twenty-seven. Around her, nurses hustled back and forth, and patients headed for the toilets, dragging IV stands along after them. She carefully repressed the impulse that struck her, not letting anyone know what she was thinking.

"............"

It was all so unnecessary. Sunlight would never normally have reached all the way to the bottom of the open shaft, but one of the biggest sponsors of the hospital's construction, Teratsuki Kyoichiro-shi, had proposed they put a garden there. Because of him, the inner walls of the smokestack-shaped hospital were lined with mirrors, bringing light to the bottom of the pit. Most of the light hit the ground, as it was supposed to, but every now and then the angles would align and send a flash into the hospital. There were sunny spots throughout the building where this was intentional, but when the beams hit her eyes anywhere else it always grated on Makiko's nerves.

The slippers on her feet clattered a little louder than normally.

"…him," she whispered, so quietly no one else could hear. "…ll him."

Despite this, she went on her way, toward the hospital room where she was to do some counseling.

Her primary role as a psychiatrist was to look after the emotional well-being of patients forced to stay in the hospital for lengthy periods of time, whether from illness or surgery. Occasionally she would also see outpatients when the other doctors' schedules were full.

She entered a private room without knocking.

There was a single man on the bed, sitting vacantly upright.

He had diabetes, and was not a mental patient, but his hollow, mindless expression looked more than a little schizophrenic.

The cold gleam in Makiko's eyes was no less insane.

"Shinokita-san," she called.

Slowly, stiffly, he looked in her direction.

"…………"

He did not answer.

"Did someone come to see you?"

"…………"

"Aw, nobody ever does," she sneered.

She moved to his side and touched him. The moment Makiko put her hand on his shoulder, the man violently convulsed. No—he shuddered.

His expression changed. His eyes opened wide, his lips half-opened, quivering, and his teeth were chattering—he was shaking with fear.

"Were you lonely, Shinokita-san?"

Moving slowly, she slid her arm around his throat.

"You worked yourself to pieces for your company, but your wife divorced you, the company demoted you, and all those years of drinking with your coworkers ruined your liver. Your company was nice enough to give you sick leave, but how long will they wait? When the insurance runs out, how will you pay your hospital bills?"

She whispered sweetly in his ear.

The man was shaking like a leaf, all the blood drained from his face, not even listening to what Makiko said.

"Augh," he groaned.

Makiko suddenly grabbed his cheeks with both hands.

"Look at me!" she snapped, yanking his face toward her.

"Eek!" The man froze, too frightened to tremble.

"Yes, more, more, fear me more, fear me from the bottom of your heart!" Grinning, Makiko brushed the man's lips with her right index finger.

She turned the finger, pointing at her own face.

Then she suddenly plunged her fingernail into her own left eye, stabbing it to the root.

"............!" The man's jaw dropped open in shock.

Makiko calmly pulled her finger out. The eyeball came with it, skewered on her finger. The nerve endings trailed along after it.

The gaping hole in her face yawned at him.

"Just a trick! A harmless little trick," Makiko whispered breezily. But no amount of makeup could create a hole in one's head.

No ordinary human could do this.

No ordinary human.

But if she wasn't ordinary…

"Hee hee hee hee," she laughed quietly, popping the eyeball back into the socket.

She closed her lid, and slowly pulled her finger out again, leaving the eyeball in place.

Her eyelid twitched back and forth a few times, and when she opened it again her eye looked just like it always had. Her iris focused—the eye was clearly still functioning, seeing.

"…eee…eeeek……!" A kind of voiceless scream came from the man's throat.

The IV in his arm popped out, his arm tightening from the sheer depth of his fear. Makiko instantly clapped her lips to the wound it left behind.

She began to slurp noisily, drinking the man's

blood. Fear had secreted other elements into his blood, and it was quite bitter. But she lapped it up hungrily.

Only when she had sucked his blood for a full minute did she slowly begin to back away.

The room had filled with a new scent. The man had pissed himself.

"Aw, *again*, Shinokita-san?" Makiko said, sneering at him once more.

"Ah…ahhh…" The man was frozen, unable to move.

Makiko reconnected his IV.

"Whatever will we do with you," she said, pressing the button for the nurse. In his ear, she whispered, "If you go crazy, you can come to my ward, Shinokita-san. Then I can taste you any time I want…"

The man twitched again. He had no way to escape. He had no choice but to live in fear.

The nurse arrived.

"Ah, did we have an accident?" she asked, and then began changing the sheets, muttering under her breath.

Makiko left the room as if nothing had happened.

"Whoops," she said, wiping a drop of her own blood from her cheek. She was careful not to let anyone see.

Looking positively placid, she muttered under her breath, "...not enough. Not nearly enough. More, much more powerfully destructive! I need that kind of fear! This is not nearly enough!"

There was a terrifying despair in her eyes, but a gleam behind it that spoke of an awful appetite.

"It is a mistake to say that humans see
only what lies in front of their eyes.
They do not even see *that*."

-Kirima Seiichi,
When a Man Kills a Man

1

"**M**akiko-san, you've been using your father's laboratory recently, haven't you?" Makiko's mother asked one day. As always, there were only the two of them at the dining room table.

"Yes, I find I can concentrate better in the lab," she answered, quietly.

"What do you do in there? Are you bringing work home?"

"A little bit. Don't worry about it. I'm not making any noise, am I?"

Makiko was not the least bit rattled. She was absolutely confident her mother would never uncover her secret.

"But...Makiko-san, you work at the hospital until late at night, and then you bring work home on top of that?"

Her mother had a horrible habit of speaking in clichés.

"I don't really have a choice. If I don't work, we don't eat."

"But, Makiko-san…"

"You really shouldn't worry, mother. I am a doctor, you know. I know full well what my body can handle," Makiko said, firmly.

"Even so, Makiko-san. It's good to be passionate about your work, but you can't be alone forever."

"That old line again?" Makiko said, annoyed.

The remainder of their conversation followed well-established lines, never getting close to anything of import.

Her mother could never have suspected that her daughter had long since given up being human.

Kisugi Makiko lived alone with her mother, who would turn sixty this year. The house was much too big for two. It had been built a generation before her dead father, and now was just big and old.

The house no longer even belonged to them. It

had long since been mortgaged to pay off their debts. But nobody had offered to buy it, and they had been allowed to continue living there, maintaining the property. They would be forced to move the moment the real estate agents managed to sell it.

Her father had been a doctor as well, and the room where he had performed his experiments was where Makiko felt most comfortable. Outside of it she was scorned, the daughter of a bankrupt family, but in the lab she was cut off from the world. In there, she felt like she had when they'd been wealthy.

So when Makiko found the "medicine" and began studying it in secret, her mother had not thought anything of it. It had never occurred to her that there was anything unusual about Makiko's behavior.

Her mother had aged very quickly after her father's death, but even so, if she had watched her daughter attentively, she might have noticed the change.

Her daughter was oddly cheerful, and there was a newfound gleam in her eyes.

It had all begun two months before, when she

had found a half-used ampule of unknown origin in a patient's room.

It was lying on the floor under a sleeping patient's bed. It looked like nothing more than trash. It was placed there so unobtrusively, like a ball lying by the side of the road outside a house.

But she had picked it up.

And hidden it away.

"…it was nothing," she had said to the guard who came running, worried that there was an intruder.

Even now, she didn't know just why she had kept the discovery a secret.

But directly afterward, the patient in the room where she'd found the medicine made a miraculous recovery from an unknown and incurable disease.

…because of this?

In her home laboratory, she carefully examined the liquid in the ampule. There was very little of it, so she had to be careful not to waste any.

When she injected a rat with a very small amount of the liquid, the most surprising thing happened.

The rat's movements doubled in speed. It demonstrated reflexes and decision-making skills three times that of an ordinary rat. And not only that—the rat's body had become incredibly resilient, nearly immortal. She could cut off its legs and arms, and it would regrow them. The phenomenon was completely unimaginable given its physical construction. The data she recorded could cause a revolution in the medical field.

...this thing is no longer a rat.

The more she experimented, the more her conclusion was driven home.

The only thing she could think was that it had evolved into something else.

The rat only died when she cut off its head. But even then, for several seconds the severed head was clearly capable of understanding what had happened to it. When she saw that, Makiko felt a shiver run down her spine. It was not a shiver of fear or revulsion, however. She knew full well this had been a shiver of exultation at the sheer power the new life form had displayed.

She did not tell anyone about the medicine.

If she told her superiors, they would undoubtedly claim credit for its discovery. That would've been unacceptable. The suspicion might have been part of her reasoning.

But she felt like it was not the *real* reason.

For reasons she could not fully understand, she believed this medicine was not something anyone else should know about.

Or, yes, perhaps by then she had already ceased to be human.

One day, Kirima Nagi, the patient who had been in the room where she found the ampule, came back to the hospital for a checkup.

"It's been a while, hasn't it, Nagi-chan?" Makiko said, calmly, when she saw her sitting on the couch outside the outpatient reception desk. It was Makiko's job to counsel patients all over the hospital, and she'd gotten to know Nagi well enough to make small talk even though she was no longer a patient.

"Yeah…you look the same," she said, absently. Nagi was the heir to a huge fortune. She was always on guard against any adults who approached her. Though she didn't really seem hostile—Nagi was only fourteen after all—she seemed quite worldly and mature beyond her years.

"I have to admit, I still don't know how you got

better," Makiko said, not bothering to beat around the bush. Nagi was much too smart to get caught by leading questions anyway. She was better off getting right to the point, expressing her professional curiosity.

"You still think it was all in my mind, Dr. Kisugi?"

"Well…yes, to tell the truth."

"Mm, well…I got to admit I've been starting to suspect as much myself."

It was rare to hear Nagi admit anything, so Makiko pounced. "…any grounds for that hypothesis?"

"Yeah. I…met someone. After that…it felt like a weight was taken off my shoulders, and I've been wondering if that was what cured me."

She spoke calmly, peacefully. It did not seem like she was lying.

…so this girl has no idea that someone might have injected her with the medicine?

It didn't seem like she did, which meant there was no point in questioning her. In fact, she had to be careful not to reveal her own cards.

"Heh…so, this someone…was it a boy?" she

said, hiding her own desire to end the conversation.

"It was a very strange man. He's gone now. Vanished into thin air. I looked everywhere, but…I don't think I'll ever find him. Not anymore."

"Hmm…" Makiko said absently, not at all interested. "Your first love?"

Nagi chuckled. "I dunno. Wonder what my dad would have said…?"

When Nagi's father, Kirima Seiichi, had been alive, he had struggled to define the shape of the human heart. Makiko had read some of his books. From a psychiatrist's perspective they were fairly slapdash, but they had a fascinating habit of hitting the nail on the head in a manner she felt sure was pure instinct.

"They say first love never bears fruit, and is soon forgotten," Makiko said, hoping the cliché would free her from this conversation.

"Yeah, I know, but somehow…" Nagi looked up suddenly, and stared at Makiko. "Dr. Kisugi, why did you become a psychiatrist?"

"Eh?"

"You see, I'm really not sure what to do with

myself from now on. So I wondered why you chose your path."

"…………"

The question had taken Makiko by surprise. She could not have explained why. *But*…

"Well…maybe I was just a coward," she said, before she knew it.

"What do you mean by that?"

"Analysis…part of it involves taking apart indescribable fears. I was a huge coward when I was younger, and always wondered why there was such a thing as fear. Maybe I ended up here in the hopes I'd be able to answer that question…"

"Hmm…then, maybe…" Nagi started to say.

But the loudspeaker came on. "Kirima-san, come to window number three."

Nagi broke off, and stood up. "They're calling me. See you again, Doctor."

She waved.

"Yes. Goodbye, Nagi-chan," Makiko said, waving back.

That was the last time they ever met inside the hospital.

…the next time they met, it would be in darkness.

Once she knew that the medicine brought about a change in living things, Makiko lost all interest in figuring out just what it was—there was something else that preyed upon her mind.

In particular, *What would happen if I injected a human?*

She did not have particularly advanced facilities, so there was no way she could try it on a monkey. The basement wasn't large enough.

So…*a patient?*

When she caught herself seriously considering the idea, it was enough to rattle her.

But we have some patients who are like living corpses. They show no reaction no matter what you do to them…

…no, no, no, no, no, no! How can I even think that?!

She wondered if she should just abandon her research and tell the world about the medicine.

But then there was the question of who had manufactured it. If a medicine this astonishing existed and no one knew about it…

It's been kept a secret.

That was the only explanation. So why was it in Kirima Nagi's room?

That question dogged her, but every time she thought about it, she always found herself thinking instead:

So if it's a secret...then can I use this without getting caught?

And use it...on myself?

Medicine that granted immortality...to her.

The idea became steadily more intriguing.

"Whenever you are hiding something
from other people the world is hiding
ten times that much from you."

-Kirima Seiichi,
The Proliferation of 'Dunno'

2

A string of grisly murders had been committed in town.

Teenage girls were being murdered, one after the other. The string of murders was noteworthy because of the manner in which they were killed.

The victim's skulls had been torn open.

The maxilla and the mandible had been pried apart, and the spinal cord had been yanked out of the head. The skin on the face had been pulled open without being pared away from the bone. Inside the head there was nothing left; everything had been removed as though a dog had cleaned it out.

Investigators could only conclude that the contents had been sucked out through the foramen magnum and other smaller natural openings into the skull.

But how?

What reasons could anyone have to kill like this?

There were various theories regarding the method of the killings, but everyone on the case agreed that the murderer must be insane.

"It's possible the killer holds some extreme superstitious beliefs about the brain, and believes he can absorb their knowledge…" droned an expert on TV.

Kisugi Makiko giggled.

"What?" asked the intern sharing the staff lounge with Makiko. Interns were generally the lowest ranking people in the hospital, constantly running errands for everyone else, but Makiko's position was not much higher, so they were on friendly terms.

"Nothing, I just thought he looked good on TV," she said dryly.

The doctor on screen was an associate professor at a large university. He had written a number of books and was often called to comment on cases like this one.

"Ha ha, true enough. If you're good looking, you don't have to actually *say* anything, as far as TV's concerned," the intern said, laughing. Then he grew serious. "Dr. Kisugi, what's your take on the case? I can't even begin to understand it…"

Makiko gave him a pained smile. "The director would advise specialists not to get interested in such extreme cases," she said.

He winced. The case was something of a taboo around the hospital. Partly because of their proximity to the murders—the police had come by asking if they had any patients who might be capable of such an act. It had caused quite a lot of disruption.

"I dunno, maybe the TV doctor's right."

"An obsession with the brain? That doesn't sound right, somehow. Maybe I've seen too many brains," he chuckled. The hospital had a number of brain samples pickled in formaldehyde. They were only about the size of two human fists, lumps of gray meat with no mystic aura around them. They were certainly nothing like the vivid objects seen in horror movies. Those props might have been able to inspire the sort of superstition they were chattering about on TV, but real brains were nothing more impressive than what you could find at a butcher's shop. That's why most superstitions tended to revolve around the skull, instead.

"But you need fairly advanced knowledge to take apart the skull like that. The killer must be using tools. That person must also be a maniac!" His cheery tone made *him* sound like the maniac. Looking at the crime scene images on TV, he added, "Maybe the damage itself is his purpose. Perhaps he enjoys breaking the skull open…what do you think?"

"No idea," Makiko said, glancing sidelong at the intern. The look in her eyes was cold enough to raise goosebumps.

Her tongue cracked like a whip inside her mouth.

He's too sweet to bother with. No matter how much I scare him, it'll never have much taste.

She could tell exactly how mentally strong other people were, now. It was as though she could reach out and touch it. No, it was more like she could reach out and *lick* it.

The stronger someone was, the more "bitter" the person would appear to her; if they were weak, they seemed "sweet."

The sensation went well beyond instinct or imagination. The knowledge was as clear and definitive as an
ice cube in the hand is cold. Her skills also made it very
easy to discover what a human's weakness was.

For example, this intern…

"But if the killer turns out to be a doctor, there'll
be no end of trouble," he said cheerily.

"Like jumping into a snake's nest," Makiko said
absently.

The intern twitched, turning to look at her. He had
gone pale. "Wh-what?!" his voice trembled.

"That's a common expression, isn't it? Or was it
a hornet's nest?" Makiko said, innocently.

He recovered somewhat. "Oh, right. Just a figure
of speech."

"You don't like snakes?"

"N-not as such," he said, breaking into a cold
sweat.

Makiko could not tell if this man had ever had a
traumatic encounter with a snake. But she could tell
that he had had some sort of sexual trauma. He had
been violated by something resembling a snake—like
a male sexual organ. Or perhaps his encounter with
that pedophile had been his first sexual experience.

Either way, to Makiko's eyes he appeared to have a snake wrapped tightly around his lower body.

What Kisugi Makiko had obtained from the medicine surpassed healing abilities impressive enough to allow her to pull out her eyeball and put it back in.

Sensing enemy strength, perceiving their weak points…these were the most impressive of Makiko's newfound abilities.

On a basic level, they were nothing more than the traits any animal needed to survive in the wild. They had simply been elevated to extreme proficiency.

Of course, she had already put these abilities to use. The hospital director was already incapable of saying no to her. She had had several of the snottier nurses fired, but had soon tired of that. She had begun to believe this ability was not to be wasted on such trivial affairs. It would be easy to take over the hospital, but she had ultimately decided against it.

True, if she used her abilities carefully, she could do anything. But she was cautious.

She had to be wary of the medicine's creators.

They would know of her ability, or of similar abilities, and have countermeasures in place. This was one reason for her caution.

But there was another reason. A side effect—the real reason she could not use her abilities openly. If her new talents became public knowledge, the entire world would be against her.

"Bad experience with snakes?" Makiko said, still toying with the intern.

Every time she said the word, he blanched. "N-no…not really. Just…they're creepy, that's all."

There was no trace of the cheer he'd displayed earlier while talking about the serial killings.

"According to the outdated theories Freud put forth, snakes are a metaphor for male genitalia," Makiko said, blithely.

The intern went white as a sheet and started to tremble. "L-like I said, it was not like…I've never…"

The tip of Makiko's tongue could taste the sourness of his fear. It was pathetically weak.

"............"

A violent urge rose up within her. She felt a sudden desire to shred the frail life-form in front of her.

She wanted to terrify him to the brink of madness and toy with him before tasting his blood. No, that was understating what she wanted—what she *needed*. She longed to stick her head right into his mouth and suck out all the chemicals in his brain.

She wanted to do to him what she did to those high school girls...

"Wh-what's happening........?"
"This is a dream, a nightmare...it must be..."
"Nothing like this was ever meant to happen..."
"Help! Somebody help........!"

Voiceless screams, death throes, and the delicious chemical secretions terror released into the body.

Human fear was the ultimate pleasure for her.
But...
But now was not a good time. If she killed this

man here, she would leave evidence behind. And even if she drove this man to the height of fear she would never get any real pleasure from it. She would have to exercise forbearance.

She acknowledged the urge as one of ravenous desperation; it would eventually demand release.

But not now.

"Are you okay? You look pale?" she said, shifting her tone and looking at the intern with concern. "You've had so many emergency patients recently…are you drinking vegetable juice?"

"Oh, the one the assistant director keeps hyping? Honestly, it's just not my thing," he said, obviously relieved that she'd changed the subject. He looked like he'd escaped within inches of his life.

Makiko, of course, knew that that was precisely true.

The stronger the better.

Makiko became aware of that principle shortly after she began her activities. The depth of flavor to the fear was not even comparable.

In the last three months, she had already taken apart the skulls of five people, and every one of them had looked to have an incredibly strong will. Checking up on them later was easy since the media was reporting their information in great detail. It appeared that all of the girls had unusual personalities. Their youth might've had something to do with their apparent fearlessness.

Makiko had little interest in pondering the matter further. It was transparently obvious, after all. She did not need to look hard to find additional prey. She could find her victims just by wandering around town.

Almost none of them were men. She began to suspect that the kind of strength she sought might not be a male trait. Men typically started shaking with fear instantly, ruining their taste. There were scores of tall, physically imposing men who, when confronted by Makiko, were no stronger mentally than an average three-year-old. The few who were unafraid were severely lacking in mental stability.

But the nice part about the unstable ones was that they were quite easy to control.

She could toy with the long term patients, nibbling at their fear, and none of them showed any inclination to fight back. It was so easy. However, such low-hanging fruit did little to sate her hunger. They were more like a snack—not truly satisfying.

All the weaker people did was fuel her desire to find the *real* thing.

But I must figure out something to do with the bodies…

She attacked when the urge drove her to it, and the aftermath was rather gruesome. If she didn't keep a low profile, whoever had made the medicine would eventually notice.

I must do something…

There had to be a good way to dispose of them.

She had to think of something safer. She needed a technique, like the contraception methods used during sex.

And she would have to frame someone else for the earlier murders. The media and police seemed to believe the killer was male, so she could easily find an appropriate scapegoat. That would keep anyone who could threaten her from hunting her down.

She chose her course of action carefully and cleverly.

But despite her cunning, she still was unsure why

the medicine had granted her new powers—along with these violent urges.

There may have been some distorted fate, a massive, unstable tendency behind the uncanny birth of Kisugi Makiko, who might well have remade the world…but there was no one on Earth who knew about it.

At least, not yet.

"I'm home," Kisugi Makiko announced as she walked in.

Her mother met her at the door. "You must be tired. I've drawn you a bath."

"I'll eat first."

They sat down at the table, just as they always did. On TV, a news anchor was providing the latest updates on the Skull Dissection Murders.

"My, how terrifying. Makiko-san, you really have to be careful out there. Such a terrible thing, and only happening to girls…" her mother shivered dramatically.

"Yeah," Makiko said, absently.

Ironically, Makiko was the source of her aging mother's weakness. The idea that anything might happen to her beloved daughter was a source of unbearable fear.

It would be so easy, so very *simple*. All she had to do was tell her mother the truth, and it would destroy her world.

It was so easy Makiko had never bothered.

"…………"

Occasionally she would glance at her mother's profile as they watched TV, and wonder what she would taste like. But she'd never done anything more than wonder. So far.

The news shifted subjects, and the president of some other country came on screen. He was surrounded by a small army of imposing bodyguards.

"…………"

Makiko could detect every one of their weaknesses. A single threat could make them all her slaves.

Recently, Makiko's abilities had begun operating on a greater scale, well beyond individual weaknesses.

She could now see holes in the policies of a large corporation, for example. Humans did not live in isolation, but in communities, and she had learned to detect what the weaknesses of those groups were. She used her newfound skills to place several organizations under her thumb. She began to use them to gather information for her.

Including some clues as to the medicine's creators.

It would not be long before she'd be able to determine the weakness of an entire nation just by looking at its president.

What would it taste like when an entire nation screamed, writhing in fear?

Maybe something even larger existed, an existence beyond her imagination.

"…………"

She said nothing to betray her thoughts, simply moving her chopsticks as her mother shook her head and complained about the state of the world.

It was not yet time for action.

"If you are a warrior, born to fight,
then the object of your life's purpose
exists only within the enemy."

-Kirima Seiichi,
Isolation and Faith

3

Kisugi Makiko sat in the hospital examining room by herself, looking at a file concerning a certain individual. There was a headshot clipped to the side, and the file looked like a patient's chart at first glance. However, this person was not staying at the hospital. In fact, she had never even been there.

She was just a girl Makiko had seen on the street.

She had been in a coffee shop, comforting a crying friend. It seemed her friend had just been rejected by a boy. But this girl was not comforting her friend with blind pity and meaningless reassurances. Instead, she patiently explained that while the boy had certainly handled it badly, her friend was partially to blame for the breakup as well. And her friend accepted

the explanation. Makiko was impressed. Most bro-
kenhearted girls were much too upset to listen to any
explanations regarding why they had been rejected. A
casual observer would not have noticed, but Makiko
could tell this girl was extremely intelligent, and very
persuasive.

And very strong.

Astoundingly so.

Imagining her quivering in fear was so exciting
Makiko almost attacked her right then and there, but
she managed to restrain herself.

She arranged for one of the men under her control
to investigate the girl. She was surprised to discover
she was still in junior high. *She's only thirteen!* The
youngest victim so far had been a high school junior.

This special girl's name was Suema Kazuko. As
with Makiko's other targets, she had a reputation for
being unusual.

"............"

Makiko could feel the desire welling up inside her
just from looking at the file. But if she killed someone
this young, the news would be all over the story. The
police and the media would go on the warpath, and

whoever made the medicine would certainly notice.

She would have to be careful.

She would have to make this girl her first carefully calculated victim.

The intercom on her desk rang. "Doctor, your patient is here."

"Okay, send them in."

She put the file away, and started playing light music, creating a relaxing atmosphere.

"Listen to me, Doctor. Everyone is saying bad things about me. All the time!"

"I think someone is following me…"

"…er. …no, well…um."

As her patients babbled on with the utmost seriousness about their absurd problems, she said nothing. She just sat in silence, smiling reassuringly. She was quite efficient as she handled each one. In the past she had tried to be as nice as possible, but now her counseling was brisk and businesslike. Strangely enough, her patients seemed to like it better.

One patient said to her, with bizarre cheerfulness, "Just between you and me, the world's about to end."

"Oh dear."

"Yes, I agree—it's a shame. There is a terrible evil lurking in the world, and it is starting to move," he said with the utmost sincerity, but he was oddly upbeat.

"Hmm…but why is it going to destroy the world?"

"That's why it was born! There's nothing else for it to do. It's merely following the instincts it was born with. It's destiny!"

He didn't seem to mind the dire fate of mankind.

"I see. How awful. I don't suppose there's any way we can stop it?"

"Of course not!" he shook his head happily.

"Then what should we do?"

"There's nothing we *can* do. We just have to give up and wait to be wiped out, writhing in fear!"

"Fear?"

"I imagine we'll all be very scared," he said, his mood only improving.

Makiko chuckled, "Sounds terrible," as if it did not affect her either.

"It will be," the patient said, like a dog with its tongue hanging out and tail wagging.

The Beach Boys' clear voices were singing "Surf's Up/Aboard a Tidal Wave" over the examining room speakers.

The final patients for the day were a junior high school girl and a young mother. The mother was a nervous wreck. She kept looking around restlessly.

"Please take a seat, Miyashita-san," Makiko suggested. Only then did the woman sit.

Her daughter remained standing.

"So. What brings you here today?"

"Y-yes. Um…well, um, this girl…um…"

"_____"

The mother glanced at her daughter with a look that could only be described as loathing. The girl was tense and very embarrassed. She couldn't believe her mother had brought her here. She seemed quiet enough, though—there were no outward signs of anything unusual.

"What about her?"

"Um…doctor…you've heard of multiple personality disorder?" the mother blurted.

Makiko grimaced. "Yes, of course." That was a foolish question to ask an expert in the field.

The mother failed to notice Makiko's tone. "Th-that's what's wrong with my daughter!" she almost shrieked.

"Now, now, Miyashita-san," Makiko soothed.

"She is! I'm sure of it!" the mother insisted, stridently.

Makiko glanced at the daughter. She was absolutely mortified and had turned bright red.

"There is a very strange man's personality inside my daughter's mind! There is! He almost killed me!"

"Mom!"

"You be quiet!" The mother snapped, hysterical. She seemed far crazier than her daughter.

"Well, Miyashita-san, I don't know what happened, but multiple personality disorder is, in most cases, a fraud. Particularly in this country—there are almost no recorded cases," Makiko explained.

The mother went pale, and moaned something, but she was too worked up for Makiko to understand a word of it.

"At any rate, may I speak with your daughter in

private?" Makiko said, concealing her irritation. She summoned the nurse, who led the mother out of the room.

When they were alone together, the daughter sighed.

"So, are you a split personality? Miss…uhm…" Makiko glanced down at the chart and continued "…Miyashita Touka?"

"So she says. Not that I can tell, but…" Touka shook her head.

The music stopped. The cassette had finished. Makiko absently switched it to the next one on the stack, and pressed play.

Classical music. *Tannhäuser*.

"Do you have any idea why your mother came to believe this?"

"…I was asleep, and my mother suddenly came into the room and shouted 'Who are you?!' and I woke up, surprised."

"You were asleep?"

"Yes. Lately, I've been wondering if I was moving around while I slept, like a sleepwalker."

"But that doesn't explain why she asked, 'Who are you?' What made her do that?"

"That's what I'd like to know," Touka sighed again.

Makiko changed tactics. "Is your mother…getting along with your father?" she asked.

Touka looked surprised. "N-not…I mean…"

"I don't think that's the only reason, but martial stress can sometimes lead to psychological problems," Makiko said, watching Miyashita Touka closely. There were no signs of anything unusual. Her main source of fear seemed to be her uncle, who had once scolded her furiously but was dead now. She was neither weak nor particularly strong.

The mother, despite being married with a child, held a violent fear of men.

"Well, uhm," Touka said, flummoxed.

"Well, I can't say anything yet. Why don't we test you first?"

"Huh? Test…what?"

"We can try and find out if you do have another personality," Makiko said, half in jest. It was her last patient of the day. It certainly wouldn't hurt to fool around a little. Besides, she was curious. She'd never met anyone who actually had MPD, just people suffering from the delusion that they did. And this girl showed no signs of having such a tiresome delusion.

"Eh…I dunno," Touka said, awkwardly.

"Your mother said…'a strange man'? Try and imagine yourself being someone like that. If you really aren't a split personality, you'll make a mistake when you try and pretend you are."

"But, I can't…"

"Listen. It is perfectly natural for every human to have more than one side to them. It is not at all easy to figure out if that is really Multiple Personality Disorder. Every girl has masculine traits, just as every boy has their feminine side. So there's no harm in giving it a try."

"I-I guess not…"

"That doesn't sound like something a man would say."

"Oh, right. Uh, why, no," Touka said, awkwardly switching to masculine forms of speech. She even tried to scowl in a manly fashion. Getting into it.

"Okay?"

"S-sure."

"So, what kind of man are you? You've been described as strange, so you must be unusual," Makiko said, grinning.

The music ended, and the next track came on.

It was the same composer, but the music had abruptly become very stirring. High pitched fanfares blazed away as Makiko waited for a response.

"Man, Woman…you may call me whichever you prefer," Touka said, her expression shifting to match the music. It was a strange expression, a sort of mocking smile.

Makiko had never seen anyone look like that before.

"Oh? Your gender is ambiguous? That is strange," Makiko said, impressed with Touka's reaction. "So why are you inside Touka?"

"I do not know that yet," 'he' said, shaking his head. "But I do know my *mission*."

"Oh? And what would that be?"

"I must avert threats to the world," he said, very serious. There was not a trace of the smile or excitement her earlier patient had displayed when discussing the same topic. This person was calm and collected.

"So you think the world's in danger?"

"Apparently it is. An enemy of the world has appeared near me," he said, shrugging. "If I do nothing, the world will be destroyed. I regret causing trouble for Miyashita Touka and her mother, but I had no choice."

"That's quite a scale you're working on," Makiko said, a little nonplussed. Touka's performance was a little too good.

But he remained unflappable.

"Not really. Threats to the world are everywhere," he said, firmly.

His brazen manner was rattling Makiko. "Are there? But you don't seem very scared," she said, to cover her confusion.

"I am not scared. Not *of you*," he said, staring right at Makiko.

Makiko gulped. She tried to detect Miyashita Touka's fear again.

But for some reason, she was unable to do so.

The music around them shifted to a peaceful movement.

"…what do you mean?" Makiko said, stiffening.

Once again, he spoke with utter confidence.

"I mean…you are an enemy of the world."

"............"

The mood of the room shifted.

They had been joking around, but that sense vanished, replaced with tension as tight as a bowstring ready to loose an arrow.

"An enemy," she said, her body tensing for flight, but careful not to let him know.

This thing...

Makiko glared at him.

What is he? Is he really...no, that's absurd.

Should she kill him?

It would not be hard. They were in a hospital, and she was dealing with a patient. A strange death could easily be covered up.

But...it still might attract more attention than she'd like. If he resisted...and their battle went beyond the privacy of the room, she couldn't predict how many other people would get mixed up in the commotion and killed. She didn't care about their lives, but the attention drawn by such an incident would be a problem.

What should she do?

"Yes, an enemy," he said, so calm she could not tell if he knew what she was thinking or not. The tension mounted even higher, until it reached a level that could only be described as murderous.

Until…

"But not only you."

The course of the conversation changed.

"To be strictly accurate, the potential to become the world's enemy lies in every human. Humans are like fuses—they can break at the slightest opportunity. Any human is capable of shaking the foundation of the world without a thought for the consequences…"

He sighed. His manner was nothing like Miyashita Touka's. He seemed to be living in a much harsher reality.

"I could be described as the natural predator of that type of person."

There was something artificial, something staged about his behavior. Makiko was relieved.

Oh…

The conversation had become very abstract. She started to relax. This was nothing but a susceptible girl's fantasy.

"If all humans are like that, then I guess that does include me."

"It does."

"But is everyone *that* dangerous? I think most people are pretty normal."

"Being normal is what makes them dangerous."

"How so?"

"If you encounter something truly unique, people with a strong sense of self can accept that calmly. But if someone is too normal, they will get swallowed by the waves, pulled along by the current. That kind of rampage is the most dangerous. People who are satisfied with being ordinary have no resistance. And…the world is not as stable as those people believe. It is always in danger. People who wish to break the wall down have no shortage of chances."

His speech finished, he stopped talking.

"…………"

Makiko said nothing either, not quite able to find words.

Only the music broke the silence.

"This is good music. Very beautiful," he said.

"Yes…nothing wasted, just simple, unadorned

beauty," Makiko said, nodding. "And…it contains no trace of fear."

"What do you mean?"

"There is too much fear in the world. It's frustrating. How great would it be if all fear were to vanish?" Makiko was speaking just for the sake of it, but to her surprise, she found she genuinely meant the words.

Even so, she could not live without fear, not now.

"I see. That is your tendency."

"That is what will make me an enemy of the world?"

"Everything has many sides. Even with an idea like the absence of fear, there is always another interpretation. For example, 'If nothing died, then there would no longer be fear.'"

He stared directly at Makiko as he spoke.

"I see," Makiko said, meeting his gaze.

He might be right. That might be the truth.

Makiko herself had no way of telling. But she could detect the weak points of individuals and organizations, and might eventually be able to detect the weakness of the world itself.

And then, would she strike at that weak point?

There was no question about it. If she got the opportunity, she would have no choice but to ride that wave.

"So when you find an enemy of the world, what do you do?"

"Kill it."

"…scary."

"I have no choice. That appears to be what I am," he shrugged.

"And you have no remorse?"

"None. I doubt the ones who become my enemies would want that from me."

"Ah. So you offer your foes a proper fight to the death? Like a duel?" Makiko said, chuckling.

"Of course. You don't agree?" he asked, staring directly back at her.

"…………"

The music was rising, building to the big finish.

Makiko found herself murmuring, "When I die, I'd like to have this kind of music send me off. Not some turgid requiem or sutra."

He nodded silently.

**"If there is such a thing as a God, then
that God would exist only in the future."**

-Kirima Seiichi,
VS Imaginator

4

"I'll prescribe some medicine for your mother as well," Makiko said.

The elder Miyashita looked alarmed. "Oh, I'm not…" she said, clearly rattled.

Before she could say anything else, Makiko jumped ahead of her.

"Oh, no, nothing serious. Just something to help you relax. The best way to help your daughter's feelings stabilize is if you stay calm."

The mother backed down without much confidence. She clearly no longer knew what was right—what was the truth.

Nobody could ever really know if they were right. No one in this world could ever know everything.

"Touka-chan, try not to push yourself too hard."

"Okay," Touka said, with a cute, girlish smile. Not a trace of shadow anywhere.

Right here and now, Makiko thought, absently. *What's to stop me from killing this girl and everyone else in the hospital?*

Their fear would be very sweet. And if she made it look like she had died as well, that would not be a bad way to conceal her identity from the world…

…but…

But it was just a thought. It would attract too much attention. She was not yet at the stage where she could act that freely.

Not yet…

"Well then."

"Yes. Thank you."

And that was all, for the time being.

When the world would be in danger…only God knew.

"God Only Knows" closed.

CHAPTER 5

Public Enemy No. 1

"Ahh…"

Seiichi was sitting alone on a park bench, staring vacantly up at the sky when a girl came over and stood in front of him.

She was about ten years old—about the same age as Seiichi's only daughter, Nagi…or maybe a year younger. She wore dark clothes, and had well-groomed long black hair parted down the middle. She was quite pretty.

Seiichi was forty three, but she stood there staring at him, unabashedly.

Seiichi looked back at her. He had been working hard on his manuscript and was absolutely exhausted—over the last three days he had not even taken the time to shave. Or change clothes.

He must have looked highly suspicious. Talking to a child might well get him in trouble, so he just stared back at her in silence. He figured she'd get spooked and run away eventually.

"............"

But the girl just kept staring back at him.

Seiichi let his chin sink to his chest, looking up at her.

"............"
"............"

Almost a full minute passed during the silent standoff.

Like a staring contest, Seiichi thought, a smile stealing onto his lips.

"Oji-san," the girl said.

"What?"

"You're going to die soon," she said, abruptly.

Seiichiro raised one eyebrow comically.

"I know," he replied, quietly.

Kirima Seiichi's novels did not sell well.

He was a very popular writer, and he put out books

almost every month, but the books Seiichi insisted were his primary work, and devoted the most energy and passion to, sold astonishingly poorly.

He also published a great number of dissertative essays and books that outlined history or classic literature, and these were the only books of his that sold. Even his biggest fans would admit to his face that they'd never touched one of his novels.

As far as he was concerned, the essays and dissertations were just a byproduct of plotting his novels, and he was simply drawing up the ideas and the data for his own purposes, but people seemed to prefer the spinoffs to the core of his work.

Why...?

Seiichi did not feel excessively upset by this, but the complete rejection of the novels he poured his soul into was a little depressing.

Yet on he wrote, almost never taking any time off.

He didn't know why he worked so hard. It was possible he simply liked writing, and it was also possible that if he stopped writing all the failures in his life would come flooding back into his mind, crushing him. Of course, it could be said that most of those failures had been caused by none other than his obsession with writing. His divorce could certainly be traced to his constant need to work.

He chose not to think about it.

His ex-wife was no longer speaking to him, but she often met with their daughter, Nagi, whom he had custody of. She seemed well. She was remarrying soon, and he was glad. He hoped she would be happy this time. He really held no ill feelings toward her. And that very lack of resentment, he mused, was probably part of what led her to say, "You never needed me."

But he had really loved her. He still did.

Even after the break-up, he had no inclination to marry anyone else. Since the divorce was caused by her affair, the court granted him the right to demand alimony, but he had no reason to do so. Really, he'd only gone through with the divorce because she had suggested it. If she had asked him to forgive her he absolutely would have.

According to Nagi, "Being with you made Mommy tired."

She was talking about him, but all he could say was, "That's a shame," like it had nothing to do with him. Nagi smiled at his response, but it must have bothered her.

When she wasn't there, he made up for the loneliness by spending even more time writing. He hadn't changed much since his wife had left.

Then one day, Seiichi received a letter.

A thin letter, in a perfectly ordinary envelope. It was hardly unusual for him to receive dozens of letters on any given day, so he was not surprised to see it. He opened it absently, and was astonished by what he read.

Dear Kirima Seiichi,

I have never written to you before, but I have been an avid reader of your books for some time. I have something I would like you to know.

I will be dead soon. Murdered.

Yes, I know. You are already assuming that I am a mental patient with a persecution complex. I understand. Honestly, I wish to God I was, but I believe I don't have long to live. This is an inescapable fact. I have noticed strange people tracking my movements. Assassins sent by the observers. How can I put this? I was born with a strange ability, and I knew from the beginning it was not a talent the world would accept. I knew that if anyone found out about it I would not live a very peaceful life.

But then I discovered your books. In one of them you wrote as follows:

"Loneliness can be your greatest gift. The more isolated you are early in life, the greater your ability to connect to a large number of people later on."

When I read that, I felt like I'd been struck by lightning. After that, I stopped hiding my ability and began letting it affect at least a small corner of the world.

However, as I feared, my decision to expose my powers did not turn out well. Not that I regret what I did, but it seems the world is determined to eradicate foreign elements like myself. I have become the enemy of modern society. I knew that I would.

So here at the end, I thought I should thank you. If I had not read your books, I would have remained isolated, living my life with a strange sense of awareness. I never really cared for that.

Why are we born?

I prefer to borrow another writer's words to answer that question—we are born for love and revolution.

I have no idea if you would have approved of my actions. But it is an undeniable fact that your words supported me. For that reason alone I am deeply grateful, so grateful that I find myself writing this letter. Thank you.

There seems little point in writing more than this. I shall take my leave now. Good-bye. I pray that you will be in good health and writing for many years to come.

Sincerely yours.

The content alone was odd enough, but even more surprising was that Seiichi had a good idea who this anonymous letter was from.

Once before, when he had been writing a script for a manga (which had been canceled due to lack of popularity) he had received a fan letter from a boy, and he recognized the handwriting. But the earlier letter had had the boy's name and address.

Seiichi quickly went through his file boxes until

he found the boy's letter, making sure. It was clearly the same handwriting. There was nothing particularly odd about the first letter, just a few simple words of encouragement.

What does it mean? He'll be murdered...?

Seiichi found the letter fascinating. No matter how unusual his readers tried to make themselves sound in their letters, he could always determine the source of their ideas. But this one felt different. The writer simply wanted to send him this message—nothing more.

Deciding he had to know more about the writer, he called his consistently idle friend Sakakibara Gen.

"Gen, are you free?"

"Basically. I pretty much always am—you know that. What, got something you need me to check up on?"

"Yeah. Something strange. I need it as fast as possible."

"Okay, leave it to me."

Gen was a martial artist, but he had stopped teaching due to deteriorating relations around his dojo. It left him free to work part-time collecting information for Seiichi. He helped out often enough to earn credit in Seiichi's books, but he insisted he wasn't the type for publicity and refused to allow Seiichi to use his name.

"Please," Seiichi said, hanging up after filling Gen in on the details.

For a while he sat in silence, thinking.

An enemy of society…?

Seiichi himself had used that phrase, somewhere in his writings. That's what bothered him most of all.

"To start at the end…he really is dead," Gen began, three days later, putting down a picture of a boy on Seiichi's table.

"…………!"

Seiichi had feared as much, but it was still a shock.

"He died a month ago. And the stamp on the letter is the day after."

"The day after…?"

The letter had gone through the publisher, so this was a normal time lag. If it had come faster, he couldn't help but wonder if he could have done something.

But Gen shook his head. "You'd never have made it in time. He'd been missing for three days before he mailed the letter."

"Missing? So he was up to something?"

"Well…" Gen shrugged, "To tell the truth, I don't believe a word of it."

"Wh-what? What does that mean?"

"No, it really might be nothing. He doesn't seem to have caused much of a fuss, and he doesn't seem to have hurt anyone."

From what Gen had uncovered, that boy's friends had all recently started getting very good grades. "And not because he'd been tutoring them or anything. They say all he did was give them a couple of pointers or rub their head. And it was more than just their grades that had improved. One of them was in an amateur band, and suddenly he started composing really distinctive songs—they all displayed similar improvements in cognitive abilities."

"…really? So…if it were me, my novels could've gotten better?"

"Yeah, basically. And if he'd come to me I might've learned how to get along with other people. Basically, it sounds like he had a knack for taking whatever skills people were struggling with and helping them make a breakthrough. The young kids I talked to were almost in tears over his loss. 'Why did he have to die?'"

"That is hard to believe. He was still in his teens, right? What was he, some sort of wannabe miracle worker?"

"Wannabe? Look, we have no way to prove it now, but it sounds like he was the real thing. And unlike most faith healers, he didn't ask for money. Also, he only helped out his friends."

"...how did he die?"

"Fell down the stairs and hit his head, apparently. There were no witnesses—he was dead when they found him."

"So he went missing...and then was found dead at the bottom of the stairs?" Seiichi frowned. "And nobody thought that was strange?"

"Nope. His classmates and neighbors all say he was a creepy kid. Nobody knew what he was think-ing most of the time, so they weren't particularly suspicious. Only his friends made a fuss. They were the ones who talked to me. His death didn't appear on anyone else's radar. And his family moved away somewhere…vanished without a trace."

Gen sighed.

"No trouble at all. And yet, it was not enough trouble…which means trouble."

"…………"

"Seiichi, this is just another hunch…but this is bad news. If you get mixed up in this, anything can happen."

"I can't write about it, then…" Seiichi sighed.

They fell silent. Neither one of them could pursue this further. There was too little to work with.

But one thing still bothered him.

Why did that boy call himself an enemy of society?

He still didn't know.

Still bothered, Seiichi went back through the letters he'd received. He found quite a few rather similar samples.

"I'm so thrilled. I think I can do now what I thought I never could."

"I've held back so long, but now I feel like I don't need to anymore."

"I have newfound power thanks to you. I have the courage to take that first step."

Until now, he had been content to know he made his readers happy, and he'd been grateful for their letters, but now he saw a common nuance lurking behind their writings.

They're all talking about what they can do, skills they didn't have before, things like that...

But what did they actually *mean*?

Belatedly, but with no better ideas, Seiichi sent letters back to them, asking how they were getting along.

Almost all of them came back undelivered.

Those that did elicit a response were always from the family. "...passed away two years ago. He was a big fan of your books..."

"............"

By this point, it was rather obvious. People who loved Kirima Seiichi's books were either dying or going missing.

What the hell is going on…?

By this point he could not even talk to Gen, his best friend. Gen had such a powerful conscience that he would pay no heed to the danger involved. If there had been even a tiny clue about the first boy, he would definitely have followed up on it.

But even he had said nothing good could come of getting involved in something like this.

Seiichi could almost smell something major operating behind the scenes.

"…………"

Thinking about it was making his stomach hurt. His nerves were fraying. Nagi noticed and had started asking if he was okay, looking worried.

"Nah, it's nothing."

"You're working too hard. You need to rest!" she wheedled, accusatively. Seiichi could feel himself calming down.

"Nah, I'm fine. Really."

"You are not! I'm serious, Dad!"

"Ha ha, sorry, sorry."

Every time Nagi got mad at him, he thought, *No matter what happens, I have to keep her out of it.*

He had no way of knowing what the future held,

and had no way of telling just what kind of destiny his daughter would eventually choose for herself.

That she would become the Fire Witch was beyond the imagination of even a writer like Kirima Seiichi.

But even with all that, his output never slowed.

Obviously, part of his drive to write was so he'd earn money and be able to raise Nagi, but above and beyond that, he simply felt like he *had* to write. He didn't know why, but the way he wrote had changed.

He stopped writing novels.

He devoted all his efforts to the kind of Kirima Seiichi works that pleased people, books that had commercial value. Hardly anyone noticed the change. His novels had always been largely ignored, and their sudden disappearance did not make much difference. Since he was still publishing more than ten books a year, he could hardly be accused of slowing down.

Then, one day at the dinner table, Nagi said

something that made him look up in surprise. "Eh? What?"

"I said, Mom wants to see you."

"…why?"

"They've set a wedding date, and she wants to see you once before then. I don't know why," Nagi shrugged.

"But I have no hold over her. I wonder why…?"

"You don't want to see her? I can tell her that."

It was hard to tell which of them was the parent.

"N-no. It's fine. Tell her I'm willing to meet," Seiichi said.

Nagi started back at him. "Dad…you're still in love with her, aren't you? You'd do anything she said?"

He flushed. "Th-that's not the kind of thing you should be asking!"

"But…ah, never mind."

"What?"

"Nothing," she said, turning away.

"Now I have to know! Tell me," he insisted.

"Okay then," Nagi said, sulking. "The man she's marrying…he's rich. A lot richer than we are."

"Huh. So?"

"So an extra child or two wouldn't matter at all."

"…………"

Now Seiichi understood.

I see...

She wanted to take custody of Nagi. That's why she wanted to see him.

"…so what do you think?"

"…what do *you* think?" Nagi countered, sounding a little angry.

"Oh…I…" He would be lonely without Nagi. But…if Nagi was taken away from him, her safety might be guaranteed.

"I…"

Nagi stared up at him earnestly.

Then she suddenly burst out laughing. "Ah ha ha ha!"

Seiichi looked back at her, surprised.

"Wh-what's so funny?"

"You looked like you were about to cry! Don't worry, I'll stay with you," Nagi promised, grinning happily.

Seiichi was taken aback. "I really looked like that?"

"It was so obvious! You really *are* green," she said, with a touch of childish bluntness. Had she learned the phrase watching samurai movies?

"Green…?" There were times when Nagi seemed to be much more of an adult than he was. "You're much more together than I am. Yikes."

"I am! Children are born later, and it is our destiny to out-evolve the adults!" she cackled. This time some sci-fi film was providing her ideas, in all probability.

"Evolve…they do say the child is father to the man."

That was an English expression, and actually meant much the same thing as the Japanese expression, "A three year old's soul lasts a hundred years," but he chose to translate it literally.

"So, by out-evolve, are you saying you plan to trample the people that came before you?" he said, taking the joke to the next level.

Nagi laughed again. "Of course! All the humans who have ever lived were just stupid, and we kids will have to teach lessons to adults instead! Ha ha!" she laughed, waving a finger around.

"So while you boast, we have to bow our heads

to you? Sounds awful. I bet a lot of people would complain…"

He trailed off, an idea striking him.

Evolution…

Of course! How had he not noticed?

That was the reason.

He had been thinking of little else. That boy with the ability to make other people's talent bloom, and all the others as well—they had all been *ahead* of the people around them.

Until now he had been wondering why such amazing people had been targeted, but he'd been looking at it backwards. They had been eliminated *because* they were advanced.

By what?

He had just said it himself. Everything in the present would resist the appearance of the future. The scale of that made him dizzy just thinking about it. Such careful and knowledgeable targeting went far beyond the level of any natural organization.

This was a war for survival. There could be no mercy. The new people would be killed the instant they showed even the slightest glimpse of themselves.

And all those people who had read his books, and decided to use their powers…

So now…

They had not yet noticed, but it was only a matter of time. When the people disposing of these evolved children noticed that they were all reading his books, they would come after him.

"…………"

Nagi glared at him. He'd tuned her out abruptly.

But she soon shrugged, and went back to eating. Seiichi often received flashes of inspiration and had a habit of ignoring the world around him.

Yet another reason I can't leave him alone… Nagi thought, giggling.

They ate in orderly silence, with none of the bustle of the moment before.

"…………"

"…………"

At length, Nagi heard Seiichi whisper, "Nagi…do you like Gen?"

"Eh? Sakakibara-sensei?" Nagi asked, not particularly bothered by the sudden question. "Sure I do. He's nice. More relaxed than you."

"Yes…I should ask him."

"Ask him what?"

"Oh, nothing," Seiichi said, resolving to ask his wife not to take Nagi in. At this stage, making any major changes would just arouse suspicions. He had to wait for it as if he knew nothing.

That would keep Nagi safe. He was a famous writer, and his death would create a stir. They would make it look natural. Which meant they would not kill Nagi with him.

This was the best way he could see to protect her.

One sunny day, in the early afternoon.

A girl was walking alone through the park. She did not have any particular destination in mind. She was just wandering.

She had a pretty face, but she liked being alone, and did not feel lonely walking around without any friends to walk with her.

She hummed quietly, enjoying the quiet beauty of the trees.

Ahead of her she saw a bench.

"......"

Her expression clouded slightly.

There was a man on the bench. He looked completely exhausted, and was staring blankly up at the sky.

She went slowly up to him and stared into his face.

He looked back at her.

They stared at each other for a while.

At last he smiled faintly, and the girl said, "Oji-san."

"What?"

"You're going to die soon."

"I know."

"You know…and you don't mind?"

"There are some things that knowing about can't prevent."

"You're not even going to try?"

"I ended up like this because I *did* do something."

"Hmm…"

It was a strange conversation, but it made sense to both of them.

The girl looked up at the sky, where the man

had been looking. "What were you looking at?" she asked.

"The birds," he said. "I was thinking about the birds."

"What about them?" the girl asked, crooking her head.

The man raised his eyebrows, and answered with a question. "Do you know why birds can fly?"

"Because they have wings?"

The man shook his head. "Because there are very few creatures that can fly. Insects and bats are about the only other living things in the air. That's why."

"Airplanes?" she asked.

The man smiled. "Those are not alive."

"So why do only birds fly?"

"If there is nothing else there, they can live without fighting. The sky is the birds' domain, and nothing else gets in their way. The birds have survived like that for a very long time."

"For how long?"

"You know about dinosaurs?" the man asked, suddenly.

"What about them?"

"Those are the birds' ancestors. At least, that's one

theory. Do you know about the archaeopteryx? People believe that birds descended from it, but some people think it was actually the reverse, and the archaeopteryx is what happened when birds were evolving into dinosaurs. Which means the birds have been around since before the dinosaurs."

It had turned into a lecture. But the girl was keeping up.

"Hmm…but the dinosaurs died out."

"There are a lot of other things on the ground. They were unable to survive down there."

"Not because of a meteor?" the girl asked.

The man laughed. "That's just a fairy tale. Even if one did fall, if it was big enough to wipe out the dinosaurs it would have killed everything else too. The dinosaurs just proved unable to compete with the other creatures. There's no other reason for it," he explained patiently. "The ones that could fly lived longer, which is very significant."

"But sometimes birds fall out of the sky."

"And sometimes it snows in April. In other words, danger and the unexpected exist for all living things equally. The question is how you survive despite them."

A dramatic way of putting things, but his tone was placid. He spoke with no trace of pretension.

"Humans too?"

"Humans, and things beyond humans," the man said, stressing the last bit. "There are things that are mostly human, but a little bit different from the humans that came before them, and they are engaged in the same struggle."

"Struggle…?"

"Everyone copes with the struggle in a different way. Some run away, some hide…and these are both ways of fighting. No better or worse than any other. They are all trying out different possibilities."

"…………"

The girl was silent for a moment. Then she asked, "Who are you?"

An ontological, fundamental question, but the man's answer was very simple, "A humble writer."

"A writer? So you're important?" the girl asked.

The man laughed. "I'm very important indeed. I may not look it, but I'm an enemy of society, public enemy number one."

He seemed to be joking, but his tone was serious.

"Enemy?"

"People who are too new for the world, and have no choice but to be its enemy, all seem to be very impressed by my books. I might as well be leading them personally," the man said, quietly, but there was certainly a note of pride in his voice.

"…so you're tempting them?"

"Maybe. But I don't really believe that much in words. If my words have given someone encouragement, then they already had the strength to follow through within them. All I've done is give them a little push, tell them they can go ahead and use that strength—that's the most that words can do. I can neither order them to take the first step nor prevent them from taking it. The words I write are nothing more than weapons—tools. How they use those weapons is up to them."

"…………" The girl thought about this for a while. Then she said, "But you're going to die."

"Apparently."

"So it won't work out. It'll end unfinished," she said, apathetically.

The man did not seem to care much either. "Nothing in this world ever works out perfectly. Everyone lives their lives making irreversible mistakes, large or small."

"Even when they know they'll fail?"

"Who decides what failure is?"

"But…if you die, you don't know what happens next."

"The will remains. Even if it doesn't look like anything but evil, if you try to do something, and seriously work to make it happen, then that will leave its mark on other people. Those people might not get there either. But what they do will be passed on to other people. And who knows? One of those people might finally reach the heart of the world…"

The man's voice faded out.

He looked up at the sky again.

"What's your name?" he asked.

"Minahoshi Suiko," the girl said.

"You can see people's death?"

"…yes," she said. She had never told anyone this before.

"Do you think that strange ability is a curse?"

"…I don't know," the girl said, with no emotion. She didn't seem to know if it was a curse or a boon.

"Nobody ever does. And nobody can ever decide

if that is a failure," the man said, staring up at the sky, not looking at her. "Whatever you choose to do with it, even if it ends before you finish, someone else after you might be more successful."

"Who?"

"It might be your enemy. It might just be a random passerby. It might even be someone who has no connection to you at all. I don't know. I have no way of telling. Nobody does."

The girl looked up at the sky herself. They stared upwards in silence.

At last the girl asked, "And you?"

"Mm…?"

"Will there be someone after you? Do you believe someone will continue what you're doing?" she asked.

"…not sure," the man said, smiling ruefully. "Truth is, I always wanted people to read my novels."

If you had looked down on that park from above, like a bird, you would have seen the man stand up, and the girl walk away again.

And thus public enemy number one met the person who'd become the enemy of the world eight years later, and parted, neither one of them knowing what the other had done or would do. The chance encounter, like all of reality, faded away to nothing.

VS Imaginator Part III –
"Public Enemy No. 1" closed.

CHAPTER 6
The Bug

1

"There's a bug inside you."

"Growing in you, eating everything you've forced yourself to forget, everything you don't want to think about."

"Your bug will decide your fate one day."

"And…chances are, you will die because of it."

"…………"

For some reason, those words came floating back into his mind.

Mo Murder had killed the boy who spoke those words several years before. The boy had a unique ability to awaken hidden talent in other people. He had been declared dangerous, an enemy of modern society. The boy said those words to him as he lay dying.

"What did you say?" the girl sitting across from him asked, frowning. She appeared to be about eighteen. She was probably not really a girl, but she looked like one.

"No…nothing," he said, shaking his head. He was wearing an ordinary suit and silver-rimmed spectacles. To anyone around him, he must have looked like an ordinary salaryman.

They were sitting in a booth in a donut shop, surrounded by high school girls and child-toting parents on their way home from shopping.

There were photographs spread out on the table between them. Well, technically they weren't photographs, but copies—printouts.

All of them featured strange images. They were of human figures lying on their side, limbs flung out like they were dancing, their mouths open wider than their heads. Looking at them led him to make the macabre discovery that human skin could stretch farther than he had previously imagined. He'd seen similar imagery in *The Mask*, but this was no movie—these were pictures of real people.

They were corpses. On each one, the skull had

been pried apart and the contents of the victim's head removed.

"…gross," Mo Murder said.

The girl laughed. "You're one to speak, assassin." He detected a hint of malice, or at least aggression, in her voice.

"…………"

Mo Murder ignored it, looking the pictures over again. He had killed enough people that he probably didn't have the right to judge the violent acts of another. Even so, this particular method of killing felt wrong to him. The wrongness seeped into the depths of his heart…

Is that why I'm thinking about what that boy said…?

The more he tried to avoid thinking about it, the more prominent the feeling would become, until it finally killed him…a chilling prophecy. He'd put it out of his mind until now.

"So? Any ideas? Why would someone kill like that? You're a killer too, you must know *something*," the girl said, trying to wind him up.

"No," Mo Murder said, honestly.

"What a shame. Well, this is your new job. Figure

out why they're killing like this, and kill the murderer if you must. You're quite familiar with ending others' lives, so this should be easy for you," the girl snapped. She clearly didn't want to be anywhere near him.

It was starting to bother him.

"Pigeon, was it? You seem a little…emotional," he pointed out.

She scowled furiously back at him. "A killing machine has no right to criticize," she said, as though she was looking at a mortal enemy.

"I understand that you do not care for assassinations, but your duties include providing backup for that kind of activity," Mo Murder said calmly.

Despite the nature of their conversation, all around them they could hear high school girls laughing and chatting. Nobody paid them any attention, so their discussion went unnoticed.

"…………"

Pigeon glared at Mo Murder, and he met her gaze with silence.

At last she looked away. "…let's talk about work."

"Very well."

This series of gruesome murders had been all over the news lately. The victims were all females in their late teens, and the method of murder—prying the skull open while the victim was still alive, and removing the contents—was so bizarre that the Towa Organization had suspected there was a reason for it beyond the current capacity of mankind to understand. Thus they had ordered an investigation. Since it related to murder, they had assigned the mission to an expert on the subject—Mo Murder.

Pigeon was a messenger, carrying orders to the agents scattered around the area. She had brought his orders along with all the information the Organization had gathered so far.

"I think I understand what I'm supposed to do. I'll start work at once," Mo Murder said, closing the file, and handing it back to her. He had memorized the contents.

She took it glumly. It would soon be destroyed.

"Where will you start?" she asked, not looking at him.

"I thought I'd begin by looking at the crime scenes. I want to figure out how they died. I want to figure out what the killer was after."

"The police did that ages ago. You won't find anything."

"There might be something that links them together, something the police overlooked. I think this killer is clearly acting with a goal in mind."

"…you sound pretty sure about that. So you'll check out the scenes, then?"

"Exactly."

Mo Murder stood up, and headed out of the shop.

"Hmph…" Pigeon watched him leave through her lashes. There was a hidden, almost snake-like darkness in her eyes.

Mo Murder's human name was Sasaki Masanori. Officially he worked in the sales department of a major food manufacturer. If anyone were to call his company (not that anyone ever would) they would reply that "Sasaki is out at the moment." He'd never even been to the place. It was unlikely he ever would.

As a synthetic human, he had the ability to release micro oscillating waves from the palms of his hands. He could use the talent to agitate a human's organs into pulp, or make a knife vibrate like a chainsaw. The only thing he couldn't cut through was armor specially designed to resist his attack. Such armor had once defeated his ability.

Even without the use of his power, he had managed to kill his target—a traitor to the organization named Scarecrow. Mo Murder's true ability was not his weapon, but his finely honed killer instinct.

"…………"

Mo Murder was investigating one of the murder scenes.

It was an ordinary park in a residential area with one slide, four swings, a sandbox, and a seesaw. Over to the side, against the hedge, was a small bench that could maybe seat four.

The first victim had been found dissected on that bench in the evening, after schools had released their students.

"…………"

Mo Murder sat down on the solitary bench. For a short period of time, the place had been crawling with reporters and rubberneckers, but that murder had occurred a month ago. Today, he was alone. The police investigation had long since wrapped up here.

Mo Murder looked around. There was nothing particularly attention-worthy about the site. There were no nearby tall buildings—just a bunch of similarly-sized houses. There was no apartment building where someone might conceivably have been watching through binoculars.

The park was on a little hill just high enough that the scene of the crime was not visible from the road. However, there wasn't a fence around it, so anyone cutting through the park would have seen *something*. If the victim had screamed, it would have drawn attention.

Which meant…the murder happened so fast she never had time to scream. But…

The murder seemed to be too impulsive for such techniques or power.

Considering the state of the body, this should have been more calculated, deliberate…but it seemed like she had been attacked without hesitation.

It was just a coincidence that no one saw them… I'm sure of that. But then, that would mean this was more like…

"A carnivorous animal out hunting?" someone said.

He looked up in surprise, and saw a girl standing there.

When he saw her face, Mo Murder gaped. It was Kirima Nagi—the daughter of one of the men he'd killed.

"Y-you're…"

"Why are you investigating this?" she asked, ignoring his evident shock.

"I-investigating? No, you must be mistaken. I'm not…"

"That's a lie," Nagi said, firmly.

She was wearing a jumpsuit made of synthetic leather, and he could not tell how old she was. Though he knew she should only be about fourteen, she looked like she was at least eighteen, and a rather grown-up eighteen at that.

"Snooping carefully around the scene of a crime, sitting down on the bench and looking to see if there are any tall buildings around, and then muttering to yourself as you try to imagine the killer's state of mind…if you aren't investigating, just what the hell are you doing? Hmm?"

He noticed belatedly that she was using very masculine speech patterns.

At the same time, he realized she had sensibilities rather like his own. She was just as perceptive as he was. The only difference between them was that he would not have spoken to someone else. Assassins never did. The only people who did that were "warriors"—people who needed to size up their enemies.

"...what does my investigating have to do with you?" he said. He already knew the answer.

And she knew that he knew. Nagi grinned. "Obviously, it relates to me because I'm investigating, too."

She was so fearless he could hardly believe she was only fourteen.

Seeing her like this, Mo Murder found himself feeling relieved. Very relieved indeed.

I'm glad I didn't kill her...

He was surprised to hear that thought cross his mind. Quickly, he said, "I've seen you before. I remember your face," he said, trying to get his emotions under control.

"Yeah, my dad was a famous writer. When he died there were pictures of me in lots of magazines," Nagi said, snorting.

☯

"Well…you're right, I *was* investigating." He handed her his card. "I don't know…I just felt like I might be able to understand what was happening here," Mo Murder said. Nagi was sitting next to him now. He was, of course, lying—after all, he could hardly tell the truth.

"An ordinary salaryman?" Nagi said, looking dubiously at Sasaki Masanori's card.

"I know, I know. It was just a feeling, and I couldn't shake it. I felt like I might have something in common with the killer…which sounds creepy, but I couldn't shake the thought."

Mo Murder was using an advanced confidence trick. By explaining something that could not be explained, the flaws in his reasoning sorted themselves out. He knew from the start that Nagi would hardly accept any normal excuse.

"…………"

Nagi looked up from his card, and stared at Mo Murder. Glared at him. Those were not the eyes of a child.

"…and you?" Mo Murder asked. "Why are you investigating?"

"I'm bored," Nagi said.

"Bored?"

"I'm not in school, so I've got nothing else to do but hang around at home. That's all."

"Why aren't you in school?"

"I was sick. Missed most of the year, so they won't let me back 'til April. I'm on a leave of absence."

"Oh…" Mo Murder nodded, accepting her explanation. "I see."

"Okay, Sasaki-san," Nagi said, standing up. "What say we investigate together?"

"Eh?"

"You can't exactly charge this to your expense account, can you? But I happen to be rich," Nagi said calmly, nothing forced about her manner at all.

"…………"

He couldn't think of a reason to say no.

That's Kirima Nagi. Why is he with her?
Five hundred meters away from Kirima, a figure

was sitting in a car parked in a position where she could only barely see the park through the gaps in the houses.

But this figure—Kisugi Makiko, a doctor working at a nearby general hospital—did not have any binoculars. With her naked eye alone, she could make out every detail of every expression of the two figures hundreds of meters away.

She had come here following the man who called himself Sasaki Masanori. On the way she had realized he was headed for the scene of the first murder, so she'd gone ahead of him to find a place where she could watch from a distance.

Of course, she was already well aware that Sasaki Masanori was her enemy—her information network extended into the Towa Organization itself.

But Nagi's presence surprised her. She didn't think there was any connection between the two of them. Considering how strong that girl's sense of justice was, she might be here on her own.

Nagi-chan…what are you playing at?

She remembered counseling Nagi when she'd been staying at the hospital. No matter how much it hurt, that gleam in her eyes never faded. Yes, that girl might well have the strength Makiko's taste demanded.

Do you want me to taste you, then, Nagi-chan...?

A diabolical smile slid over the lips of the monster now known as the Fear Ghoul.

2

 hree years had passed since Mo Murder killed Kirima Seiichi.

It had been an easy job.

Kirima Seiichi spent most of his time at home alone, working, so all Mo Murder had to do was sneak into the house, move silently up behind him as he worked, press his palm against Seiichi's back, and send a shockwave into his organs.

Kirima Seiichi fell over at once, leaving his partially written manuscript on the table.

And just as Mo Murder was about to finish him off, he heard a key turn in the front door with a loud click.

His data had mentioned a daughter, but she should've been at school. For some reason, she had come home early.

"_____!"

For an instant, Mo Murder debated killing her too. But…

"I-if my daughter…dies too…the news will explode. You don't…want that."

He turned around at the voice, and saw Kirima Seiichi glaring up at him, dying in horrible pain.

"………"

His strength of spirit took Mo Murder by surprise. Even more surprising was the fact that the man was right.

"You knew?"

He was prepared to die?

"_____"

Kirima Seiichi just glared up at him. For another moment he debated whether or not he should finish him off.

But then a bright voice echoed through the house. He didn't have time.

Mo Murder hid himself in the library, next door to the study. He heard footsteps on the stairs.

And then she spoke. "I told them I was sick and came home early!" The daughter, Kirima Nagi, then in the fourth grade, opened the door.

She screamed. A large portion of the room was covered in the blood Kirima Seiichi was coughing up.

Nagi ran over to him.

"…………"

Mo Murder watched closely from the next room. He was ready to jump in at any moment.

Kirima Seiichi grabbed his daughter's hand.

"Nagi…what do you think being normal means?" He babbled a few more things that made no sense to Mo Murder, and then passed out. He never woke up again.

He didn't once mention the Towa Organization, or that he had been assassinated.

Nagi ran to the phone to call an ambulance.

Mo Murder slipped out, leaving as unobtrusively as he had entered. As he walked away, he could hear the commotion starting.

If Kirima Seiichi had said so much as a word about him to his daughter, or even told her to run, he would have killed Nagi, too. But that had not happened.

That man had conquered his own fear of death, protecting his daughter to the bitter end.

Mo Murder had his orders, and did not feel any remorse over killing him…but he secretly respected the man's strength of will.

And now, Nagi, spared by the flow of events, stood before him again.

Like some twist of fate…

What else could he think?

"Um, Kirima-san?" he said.

Nagi was on all fours, inspecting the ground. She looked up at his voice. "What?"

They were at the second scene now. The body had been found in a heap below a bridge, cars zipping by on the road overhead.

Unlike the first scene, where only luck had kept the murderer and the victim from being seen, this place was almost always deserted.

Nagi had paid for a cab to bring them as close to the site as possible. They had walked the rest of the way.

"I don't think there's any evidence left. The police must've collected all of it. That's why the crime scene tape was gone."

Nagi didn't answer. Instead, she looked around her, muttering, "What could it be?"

"What?"

"Sasaki-san, you can imagine the killer's state of mind, right? This place is nothing like the first one, but can you sense anything it has in common?"

"Well…" Mo Murder said, looking around. What Nagi was doing was exactly the same thing he had been planning on doing.

"This place seems like a much better choice than the last one…"

"Yes. But why?"

"Why what?"

"The murder itself was exactly the same. Why would they do exactly the same thing first in a place where they might be seen, and then in a place where they can take their time?"

"…………"

Mo Murder fell silent. That was exactly what he had been thinking.

"Why do you think?" Nagi asked again, standing up and turning toward him.

"…the killer just didn't care?"

"Didn't care if someone saw him?" Nagi asked, looking right at him. "You mean he paid no attention to who was around?"

"Maybe he thinks he's a god? That he's untouchable. Still, he seems to have rather advanced medical knowledge to believe something that crazy. This killer is very well educated, like a doctor. Then again, it's not as though elitism hasn't produced some distorted ways of thinking."

"What about you, Sasaki-san? If you had a reason to extract the contents of someone's skull, would you care if someone saw you?"

"Mmm…" he started to think about it, and then it hit him. Nagi was glaring at him. Mo Murder finally realized what she was driving at.

She suspected him, too. She was *interrogating* him.

Her reasoning might've been based on the notion that the killer always returned to the scene of the crime, but either way, she clearly suspected that Mo Murder might well be a killer himself. And she was bringing him with her. Watching him, to see if he would slip up.

"…I doubt it. I said earlier that I *might* understand, but if it were me, I'd hide the body somewhere and take my time. I'd be afraid of getting noticed. Afraid of the trouble that would cause."

He answered honestly.

"Afraid…?" Nagi whispered, looking away. "Afraid…" she said, looking around. "The killer wasn't afraid at all, you mean? Not…afraid. Not scared. No fear. Fear? Where have I heard that before…?"

She was muttering to herself now. She folded her arms, thinking hard.

"Are you onto something?" Mo Murder asked.

But she shook her head. "…nah. Next one?"

The third scene was in a back alley, and was still sealed off. Police were everywhere. Two weeks had passed since the murder, but the investigation did not appear to be getting anywhere.

"…guess we can't get in," Mo Murder said, watching them from a distance.

"…Sasaki-san," Nagi said suddenly. "You ever pick up a girl?"

"Huh?"

"You know, start flirting with a complete stranger."

"N-no, not…never."

"There's a first time for everything. See that girl standing over there? Talk to her," Nagi said, pointing at a high school girl standing perfectly still outside the police blockade.

"What about?"

"Just do it. Tell her you want to talk, bring her this way."

"…huh." He didn't know what she was up to, but Mo Murder did as Nagi asked, and went over to the girl. "Um, are you…?"

The girl jumped, and spun around.

"Wh-what?!"

"No, I…" Mo Murder stammered. She looked like a frightened rabbit, and he had no idea what to say to her. But he awkwardly managed to ask, "Why are you standing here?"

"_____"

The girl didn't answer. She looked tense.

"D-do you have something to do with the girl who was killed here?" he tried.

"_____"

"Look, I'm not anyone to be afraid of…"

That was a complete lie, but Mo Murder said it

anyway, all the while wondering just what in the hell he was doing.

"…what do you want?" the girl asked, at last.

"Er, um…"

"We're looking for the killer too. Mind talking to us?" Nagi's voice came suddenly from behind him. Mo Murder jumped. How long had she been there?

But the girl's eyes brightened at once. "The killer?" she asked.

Mo Murder was even more surprised.

The girl's name was Rika. She was a friend of the girl who'd been killed.

"How old are you?" Rika asked Nagi, as they sat down in a nearby cafe.

"Twenty-six," Nagi said without a moment's hesitation. Mo Murder almost fell out of his chair.

"You look so young…less than twenty," Rika said, not doubting her in the slightest.

"I get that all the time," the fourteen-year-old lied, smoothly.

Once again, Mo Murder was amazed by Nagi's self-possession.

"You said you're an…insurance investigator? Investigating…what?" Rika asked.

Nagi turned to Mo Murder expectantly.

"Uh, um. Well, how can I say this…the amount of insurance money we have to pay changes if the murders were random, or if the victims were pre-selected targets—if the motive was a deep-seated grudge, for example."

These were not words his false identity was likely to say. He was making it all up.

"A grudge? Shizue would never…"

"That's what we're investigating. It was an example, just an example. It *is* possible one of the other victim's families is trying to make it look like the killings are indiscriminate."

"That's just…" Rika gasped.

"If that were true, it'd be unforgivable, right?" Nagi added. "So…could you tell us what you know?"

"But I don't know…"

"What kind of person was Shizue-san? You sounded like you couldn't imagine anyone hating her…?"

"Yes, right. She wasn't the type to make enemies. Really."

"She was outgoing?" Mo Murder asked.

Rika nodded. "Cheerful, considerate…occasionally a little strict, but that was just because Shizue was so strong."

Nagi frowned.

"Strong? Strong how?"

"Oh…I don't mean she had a lot of muscles or got in a lot of fights. Just…how can I describe it…her feelings were very direct?"

"She was strong mentally? She could be relied upon?"

"Yes, that's right."

"Strong…strong…" Nagi muttered, lost in thought.

Mo Murder had no idea what she was thinking, so he continued to question Rika on his own.

"Did she spend much time alone?"

"No. No more than anyone else, at least."

"So she just happened to be alone the day she was attacked?"

"…I guess," Rika said, tearing up a little. If she'd

been with her friend, she believed, she might still be alive.

This flustered Mo Murder. He had no idea what to do with a crying girl. When someone died, the people left behind would cry, so he tried not to think about it. Knowing this, as an assassin, was a constant source of pain. He quickly changed the subject.

"Was she a leader? Did a lot of folks follow her?" he asked, glancing at Nagi. He was certainly following *her*.

"No, she wasn't like that. It was more like…if everyone was planning on going to one place, and she wasn't interested, she would say, 'I'm out,' and head home on her own. Like that."

"I see."

That sounded like something Nagi would do. Were all the victims the same type as Nagi?

If that's true…then Nagi might be on the killer's list too.

Mo Murder found the thought made his blood boil. He could not bear to think it.

Why? Do I think she's my prey? Do I not want anyone else to have her?

It baffled him.

"Something wrong?" Rika asked. Before he could even shake his head, Nagi jumped in.

"So, Shizue was not the type to be easily scared?" she asked, pointedly.

"N-no," Rika said, a little overwhelmed.

"Did you ever see her scared?"

"N-no…now that you mention it, never."

What's she asking?

Mo Murder had no idea what she was driving at.

"Then…if she were to be afraid, what might scare her?"

"…I-I couldn't…"

"Couldn't begin to imagine. So she was *that* strong."

"Y-yes."

Nagi did not seem to be asking questions so much as merely confirming the answer she had already arrived at.

"…was there a physical exam at your school recently?"

This question came out of the blue.

"Eh? Y-yeah, there was, but…"

"Was one of the doctors a young woman?"

"…come to think of it, yes. She was there in place of our usual physician…"

"Okay then," Nagi nodded, and abruptly stood up.

Without another word she ran out of the shop.

"——?!"

Rika and Mo Murder stared after her. Despite his surprise, he recovered quickly. "S-sorry about that! I'll get the check!"

He hurriedly slapped a ten thousand yen bill on the table and ran after her.

Rika was left sitting alone, stunned.

What had just happened escaped her, but for a moment, in the eyes of the girl who had claimed to be twenty-six, she had seen a look she'd seen just once in the eyes of her dead friend.

That look had come when a teacher screamed at Rika for something she'd had nothing to do with. The accusation left Rika in tears. Shizue had hissed, "Unforgivable!" and gone running off to demand that the teacher apologize. Ultimately, not only had the teacher not apologized, but Shizue had ended up getting thoroughly scolded herself, but she had remained furious to the bitter end.

"You did nothing wrong! It makes me so mad!" she said, angry for what had happened to Rika.

When she went running out of here...her eyes were just like Shizue's.

Like she was angry in the dead girl's place, unable to forgive the horrible things done to her.

"Hey, wait for me!" Mo Murder called, barely managing to catch up with Nagi. He grabbed her shoulder.

"…………"

She turned back to him, but did not answer.

"What's going on?"

"I remember! She said she 'wondered why there was such a thing as fear.'"

Mo Murder didn't follow.

"Huh? What?"

"Yes…this was never about whether the killer was scared. It was about the victims. *That* was the motive! It was the victims who weren't afraid of going somewhere deserted. The killer didn't choose the place; she chose *them* because of their strength!"

"H-hang on…what are you talking about?"

"And the medical knowledge…the higher education…and more than anything else, she'd need to be able to do the research…it's more than possible!"

She brushed Mo Murder's hand away, turning to leave.

"H-hey, wait! What the…"

"You're no longer a suspect, Sasaki-san."

"Eh?"

"I'm sure you noticed, but I did suspect you. But not anymore…which means this is goodbye."

"……!"

She put it so bluntly that it floored him. "Wh-what cleared me?"

"When I told you to talk to Rika-san, you were flustered. If you were the killer and just acting, you'd have slipped up then. But you remained a nice guy, and were flustered in the normal fashion, and clumsily went about doing something you clearly weren't ac-customed to. The killer would have relished the per-formance. And there was none of the phony behavior you might get with that. You were simply…awkward. That was enough for me."

Mo Murder tried to ask again, "B-but I'm…
I'm…"

"What, you think you could *kill* someone? That's
just an impulse, Sasaki-san. The bug inside you,
squirming. You're really a very nice man. You might
think that's ridiculous, but you would never kill anyone of your own accord."

"B-but I…" *killed your father!* he almost blurted,
but caught himself just in time.

Nagi grinned at him. "Bye!" she said, and left
with a wave of her hand.

"…w-wait! You…you know who the killer is?!
You're going to fight them?!"

There was no answer to his call. Nagi simply
walked away, without so much as a glance backwards.

3

"Heh heh heh…"

In the darkness, the Fear Ghoul laughed.

Everything was playing out as she had planned. Kirima Nagi had clearly figured out that Kisugi Makiko was the killer. Even if she wasn't completely certain, she was clearly eying her as a prime suspect.

But she had expected that. Obviously, she had remembered that when she was still human, she had once let her own fixation slip when talking to that girl. She knew things might turn out this way eventually. Nagi was smart, and the Fear Ghoul never underestimated her opponents.

But…you have no proof, *do you, Nagi-chan?*

If she went to the police, there was not a single

scrap of evidence that could lead to her arrest. Even if there was, she had a large number of policemen under her control.

Nagi did not know that, but even so…judging from her personality, her sense of responsibility, she would come in person. And alone.

"Heh heh heh heh…!"

She was ready for her.

It would not be long before that girl's incomparable strength would be hers to play with…

Mo Murder followed Kirima Nagi.

It was easy enough. Nagi might be unusually observant for a child, but no matter how closely she paid attention, she was just a human—Mo Murder was an expert at hiding and tracking, and had been born to do nothing else. If he put his mind to it, he could follow anyone without their ever noticing.

Nagi first went to an apartment building—presumably her home. Mo Murder had no way of knowing, but it was where Sakakibara Gen had lived. He had signed it over to her when he left Japan.

She soon came out again, with a bag over her shoulders.

What's in the bag? Surely not a weapon of some kind?

Given Nagi's track record so far, it seemed like a distinct possibility. She might really be planning to fight the killer in person.

Fool! What you're about to fight isn't even human!

He longed to tell her. But from a mission standpoint, allowing Nagi to draw the killer out would give him a distinct advantage. From that standpoint, what she was doing was ideal.

But.

But…argh…damn it!

Mo Murder found himself tortured by anxiety he did not fully understand.

Nagi jumped aboard a touring bicycle and sped off at a speed rarely obtained without a motor. She even had her helmet on. Such a well-prepared young woman!

Where's she headed?

Following behind, Mo Murder desperately tried to determine how Nagi had figured out the killer's identity. No matter how he examined the evidence, he still had no idea who was behind the murders. Perhaps Nagi knew something he didn't, but he had been with her the whole time. He was an assassin, an expert at investigation, yet he had not even grasped the slightest hint of the identity of the killer.

She said the "motive" was key...

He did not understand what she meant. Come to think of it, despite all the people he had murdered, he had never once thought about *why* people killed each other.

"There's a bug inside you."

"The bug inside you, squirming."

Nagi's voice, and the voice of the boy he had killed, echoed together inside his skull.

What bug?!

Everything about those two was different, but they had said almost the same thing.

He did not know it…but one of Kirima Seiichi's books, *When a Man Kills a Man*, contained the following words: "Humans do not possess a single, focused will. In their hearts, they have countless bugs, buzzing in all directions. There are times when all these bugs pounce on the same food, but when they are focused on different desires, people take actions that can only be described as incoherent." Both of them had taken the phrase from that passage.

Why? Why?

Nagi sped through back roads, reaching her destination almost completely unseen.

Once again, Mo Murder was surprised.

This was the hospital where Nagi had once stayed…and where he had attacked the Towa Organization traitor, Scarecrow.

Nagi removed her helmet, and sighed.

The sky was already dark. The sun had set, and a full moon shone in the sky. Gray clouds, bathing in the moonlight, drifted from the east.

Nagi glanced up at the building above her and then headed around the back. The front entrance already had a sign placed in front of it that read, "Visiting and examining hours are over for the day."

At the back entrance she found a security guard

and the head of maintenance. They looked surprised to see her.

"Nagi-chan, what brings you here?"

"Nothing major," she said. She'd been here long enough to know them both.

"Visiting hours are over for the day…"

"Oh, no—I'm supposed to meet Dr. Kisugi. You mind calling her?"

"No problem," the guard said, picking up the phone. "Uh, Dr. Kisugi? Kirima Nagi's here, says she wants to talk to…oh, yes. Okay. Absolutely. Nagi-chan, go right up."

"Thanks."

She wrote her name on the night visitors log, putting "private business" down in the "purpose of visit" field, and went inside.

The lights were dimmed in the halls at night, and her footsteps echoed softly.

Nagi knew the layout well. She headed right for the elevators and pushed the call button.

Mo Murder watched Nagi step onto the elevator

from the shadows, having snuck inside while she spoke with the guard.

What floor is she going to?

Without a sound, he ran up the stairs near the elevator shaft, stopping when it did.

His eyes paused on the "Psychiatry" sign.

"………?"

What was she doing *here*?

Nagi stepped out of the elevator. She crossed the lobby, moving purposefully.

He followed, making himself unnoticeable. Peering ahead, he saw Nagi stop in the smoking corner. There was a woman sitting on the sofa who stood up and called out to Nagi, stopping her. She wore a white coat. *Must be a doctor.* Probably the "Dr. Kisugi" Nagi had mentioned. In the low lighting, he could not make out her face from this distance.

"_____"

"_____"

They were speaking in low voices—nothing unusual considering they were in a hospital at night—and even Mo Murder's exceptional hearing could not pick it up. There was some machine humming nearby drowning their voices out.

He wanted to get closer, but there was no way to do so and stay hidden.

Nagi seemed a little worked up. The doctor was shrugging and shaking her head, trying to soothe her.

"_____"

At last Nagi shook her head and came back. They were done talking.

She went past the boiler room where Mo Murder was hiding, and summoned the elevator again.

Mo Murder decided to head for the stairs, keeping ahead of her. But just before he stepped out of his hiding place, he noticed the doctor staring at Nagi.

"_____?"

Something seemed wrong.

With her watching, he couldn't leave. While he hesitated, Nagi stepped onto the elevator, and it began to descend.

At last the doctor looked away. But what she did next was even stranger.

She ran to the window over the entrance, and opened it. She leaned all the way out, and stared down at the ground below.

Then she came back to the smoking corner, bent over next to the sofa, and reached underneath it. When he saw what she pulled out, Mo Murder was stunned.

It was a rifle. She assembled it quickly, and then carried it back to the window. She pointed the barrel downwards, aiming carefully.

At who? Not at Nagi?!

Any second now, Nagi would be leaving below that window, heading for her bicycle in the parking lot. Right past where the doctor was aiming.

But if she uses a gun here, someone will notice… he started to think, but his experience as an assassin soon told him that this was not the case.

For example, what if the gun was firing tranquilizer darts shaped like small hypodermic needles?

Nagi would collapse if one hit her. The guards would come running at the sound. When they lifted her up, they would see the needle lying next to her, but those were hardly unusual in a hospital. They would ignore it and take her inside to the emergency room. And the doctor who would come to look at her…

"———!"

She could pull this off. There were countless ways to kill people. Mo Murder knew that better than anyone.

He could see the doctor's face in the moonlight.

Her lips were twisted, smiling.

When he saw that, Mo Murder felt like a steel pole had been rammed through his chest.

"Ack…"

Why had Kirima Nagi, who had only known him a few hours, told him with such confidence that he could never kill anyone of his own accord? He had killed countless people.

"Augh…"

Why had Kirima Seiichi been able to make such calm and rational choices even as he lay dying?

"Aaaaaaauugh…!"

Why did this bother him so much, why was he standing in his hiding place panicking, why?

"Aaaauuuuuuuuuuuuuuuuuuuugghhhhhh!" he screamed, and threw himself toward the doctor.

Mo Murder was on her before she even turned around. He thrust his knife deep into her mid-section—it was a fatal blow.

Damn it!

His orders were to identify the killer. Killing her was secondary. But he had done it anyway.

He looked up into the doctor's face and lost track of what he was thinking.

"Eh?"

He knew this woman's face. Woman? She didn't look like a woman—she looked like a girl, about eighteen…

And she was grinning at him, even with his knife buried in her. A grin filled with murderous fury.

"Consider this revenge for Scarecrow!" said the Towa Organization's synthetic human, Pigeon, as she coughed up blood. She grabbed Mo Murder's body, holding him immobile.

"……!"

Mo Murder quickly tried to turn around. But he was too late. Someone else was coming swiftly up behind him, soundlessly.

Unable to dodge, an overhand blow struck Mo Murder from behind, splintering his spine, pulping his organs, and breaking all the way through the other side of his body.

"…guh…gah…?!"

He just managed to turn his head and look behind him. Kisugi Makiko, someone whom he had never met, stared down at him with a look so haughty it was longer human, but that of an all-powerful god.

"Hello, Mo Murder-san…and good-bye," Fear

Ghoul said coldly, and swung Mo Murder's body into the air, tossing Pigeon away across the floor.

Then she flung Mo Murder out through the open window.

As he flew through the air, all Mo Murder could think about was the boy he had killed, and his sad face.

"…I warned you, didn't I?"

And then he hit the ground.

"Dr. Kisugi just went downstairs," the young female doctor said when Nagi went to see her. She went outside, where Kisugi Makiko should have been.

But there was no one there.

"…………"

Nagi never once let her guard down. Her body was tense, well aware that this might be a trap. Though she was alert, what actually happened was still able to stun her.

Someone fell from above, right in front of her.

"____?!"

He hit the ground, bounced once, and did not move again. A pool of blood formed under him.

He was not bleeding because of the fall. There was a huge hole already opened through the middle of his body.

And his face…

"S-Sasaki-san?!"

Nagi tried to run to him, but someone else hit the ground in front of her.

However, this person did not fall—instead, she had *jumped*. The person landed from more than ten meters above, with no damage to her legs at all. Upon landing, she stood upright easily.

No human could do that.

It was Kisugi Makiko.

Nagi gasped, and the Fear Ghoul grinned wickedly.

"Sorry to keep you waiting, Nagi-chan," she said, waving her hands as if declaring her innocence. But her hands were covered in blood. The victim lying behind her explained where the blood came from better than any words.

"…………!"

Nagi could feel cold sweat running down her back.

4

"A Scarecrow and a Pigeon? Not the best couple."

"It's crows that can't stand scarecrows, not pigeons."

Ultimately, it must have been love.

Pigeon only knew Scarecrow through work, but she loved him—very much. She did not realize what that love had meant until he betrayed the Towa Organization, and was killed.

Taking care of Scarecrow's office and apartment had been left up to her, and she had cried the whole time. At times she cried so much she wasn't even sure why she was crying. The loss was so overwhelming, she feared that if she faced it directly she might go mad. Looking back on it now, that might have been a better choice than the one she made. Still, she remained alive, and carried out her duties like she always had before.

She was able to do that, but she could not shake the grief. She could not bear the thought that Scarecrow's death had, ultimately, had no real effect on her life. She had loved him so much!

When her duties required her to contact Mo Murder, the very man who had killed Scarecrow, she felt a fiery anger boiling over inside her.

And then...that woman appeared.

"I know how you feel," she said. "That's why I'm going to give you a chance."

She asked what the woman meant.

The woman laughed. "Is it not a beautiful thing to die in pursuit of revenge?" she asked.

She was terrifyingly good at getting what she wanted by working her way into the weaknesses in people's hearts.

Pigeon had done as the woman said. She had acted as bait, drawn him to her, and used her life to prevent Mo Murder from dodging the woman's attack.

And indeed, she was now dying.

"............"

The cold hospital floors were sapping all the heat from her body. The world seemed so very cold, and was gradually going dark.

Yet Pigeon did not regret what she had done. She had taken the side of an enemy of the Towa Organization. She was just like him now. She felt completely at peace.

Her face could no longer form expressions properly, but there was an approximation of a smile forming on her lips.

Because there was a shadow standing before her.

Ah…

The shadow wore a dark colored hat and cloak. It looked less like a person and more like a pipe.

Scarecrow…you came!

If she had looked closer, she would have seen that this shadow was shorter than the man she had known, and that its shape differed from his, but she was beyond the ability to make such distinctions.

"…………"

The shadow said nothing.

Tell me, Scarecrow…will I…go to heaven? she asked the shadow, utterly at peace.

But the shadow answered firmly, "No." Rather coldly. "You're going to hell."

"_____"

Surprised, she was briefly stunned, but soon…

Of course I am…just like you…

She nodded, smiling what must have been the most beautiful smile she had ever produced.

All of that had happened in her mind alone. Pigeon's expression remained exactly as it had been the moment she'd been flung aside. Her neck was twisted, and did not move. She lay on the floor with her limbs thrust out askew.

She never once moved, never once responded.

"…………"

A shadow looked down at her.

It was the only thing that remained just as it had been in her vision. Black hat, black cloak, a strange, inhuman silhouette.

"…………"

The shadow stared at the corpse for a moment longer, but then it turned…and was gone.

Nagi's reaction was frighteningly fast.

She ran without a glance behind her, jumped onto her bicycle, kicked the ground, and was pedaling at top speed a moment later.

"…mmm!"

The swiftness of her movement surprised Makiko, but she soon gave chase.

Her legs were still evolving, but they could already reach speeds of more than fifty kilometers per hour.

…she chose to run away?

Glaring after Nagi, Makiko felt like she'd overestimated her. But she soon changed her mind.

Oh…she doesn't want the security guards joining in. She's drawing me away to protect them. I see, well done.

She grinned. Kirima Nagi would be the ideal prey.

The idea had crossed her mind, but Nagi had not really believed Makiko would come running after her. Nagi gritted her teeth tightly, trying to stop them from chattering.

Try as she might, she could not pull ahead of her pursuer. Their speed was identical…no, she realized that the thing chasing after her was probably not at full speed. She was merely following her prey, waiting for Nagi to tire. Like a wolf chasing a deer.

What now?

There was a three-way fork in the road ahead, and for a second she hesitated.

Should she head toward a populated area? Maybe the police could help…

No…that was out of the question. Nobody would believe her, and the monster behind her would kill them before she could even try to explain.

Think! What now?

Nagi leaned her body abruptly to one side, taking the road into the mountains, away from innocents.

From behind her came a sound. "Ah ha ha ha!" Loud laughter. "Beautiful, Nagi-chan! You really are Kirima Seiichi's daughter. Taking the future of all mankind on your little shoulders, are you?"

The shrill voice seemed to stab her in the back. Nagi shuddered.

What now? No, I just have to grit my teeth and do it!

She turned her bicycle off the road and went down the grassy bank. It was a steep slope, and the bike tumbled precariously as Nagi clung to it in desperation.

"____!"

Fear Ghoul bounded after her with a sneer of a smile on her face.

What, you thought that little burst of speed would let you get away?

If she had thought the steep slope would make her go faster, then she was mistaken. Placing herself below Makiko only meant...

"Ha!"

With a cheerful shout, the monster kicked off the ground, leaping into the air.

Twisting as she fell, she hurtled past Nagi as though she was leaping down a flight of stairs several steps at a time.

As she landed, she turned back toward Nagi.

Nagi's eyes were opened wide but she did not even have time to brake. The monster's arm swung once, crushing the front wheel and knocking her sideways.

"Augh!"

Nagi rolled helplessly across the ground, reflexively breaking her fall like Sakakibara Gen had taught her.

She jumped to her feet hurriedly, but Kisugi Makiko was already right on top of her.

She ran, but she had not been able to get away on a bicycle, so she could hardly expect to do so on foot…

"Hee hee hee hee……! Go on, Nagi-chan, scrabble, scramble, more and more! Pathetic!" The high-pitched laughter followed right behind.

Nagi was running out of breath. Her body was no longer steady, rocking side to side as she ran on.

Yet her eyes remained the same, filled more with anger than with fear, glittering with power that her current predicament had not been able to diminish.

Kisugi Makiko could sense Nagi's fearlessness.

Even now, there was something in Nagi stronger than her fear. Makiko couldn't tell what it was; she could only discern fear. She had no idea what the other emotion was. Her prior victims had all become terrified much faster.

The indomitable warrior? Even so...

At first she had been looking forward to destroying something so strong, but now that Nagi was showing so few signs of fear even while in mortal peril, she had moved beyond Makiko's comprehension.

"............"

Makiko stopped for a moment.

Nagi realized this quickly, from the sound, and glanced back. She was calm. She knew exactly what was going on.

"............!"

When she saw Nagi's eyes, Makiko felt the blood rushing to her head. What *was* she?

I thought fear was a universal absolute! But it means nothing to her? No, that's impossible!

Even she must crumble before complete, overpowering fear!

"Enough screwing around!" she shouted. She kicked a pebble lying near her feet. It flew with astonishing speed and accuracy and struck Nagi on the right thigh.

"_____!"

Nagi fell over, sliding through the mud and right into a puddle from the momentum. The bag on her back opened, spilling its contents. There was a weapon—some kind of a nightstick—and several different kits in the water.

She flailed her limbs, trying to get out, but her leg was numb and her body would not respond properly.

She tried to move forward anyway, but Kisugi Makiko was already standing in front of her.

"…………"

Nagi backed away, but Makiko stepped forward, maintaining the same distance.

Nagi's back came up against a tree behind her. She could move no more.

"…………"

She considered moving to the side, but then she saw a look in Makiko's eyes. She knew that either way she moved she would be attacked instantly.

Nagi stopped moving. Her lower body was in the muddy water, both hands beneath the surface.

"…………"

She glared fiercely up at Makiko.

Makiko's face twisted so violently she could almost hear it.

"…fear me!" she snarled.

Nagi did not react.

"I told you to fear me! Scream! Cry! Beg like a pathetic worm! Panic!" Makiko shrieked, hysterically.

"............"

Nagi's expression never changed.

Makiko's scowl grew deeper, but then she had an idea, and her grin returned. "Oh, right...I didn't tell you about Sasaki Masanori yet, did I?"

Nagi's cheek twitched. When she saw that, Makiko gave a satisfied nod.

"You may not have known it, but...he wasn't human. He was like me. Well, he was a little different, technically, but the same kind of thing. His real name was Mo Murder. His employer ordered him to investigate me and to kill me if circumstances called for it. You see? He was *an assassin*. He's killed dozens of people. Ha ha ha! You can't judge people by their appearances. Especially when they aren't even people!"

"............"

At last Nagi groaned.

"You think I'm lying? Aw, too bad. It's all true. That man was using you, but I was one step ahead of him. Because you stuck your nose out, I was able to polish off a powerful enemy. I owe you one," Makiko said, with a distorted smile.

"…………"

Nagi lowered her head, but even now, she was not afraid. Nagi's weak point, which Makiko could sense, remained the same, unchanging.

It was "the death of someone important to her."

Dying herself was far better than having that happen, and it was her one great weakness.

That's why Makiko was so annoyed. This left her with no real way of getting at Nagi.

Was Sasaki Masanori important to Nagi? That hardly seemed likely. He was a stranger, someone she had just happened to run into, but it must have damaged her a little. His betrayal more than anything, probably. Nagi might not be scared yet, but she was rattled.

"I'm going to turn Sasaki Masanori-san into the serial killer. Instead of me, of course. Pigeon already placed all the evidence needed in his house while he was out looking for me! Ha ha, he *was* an assassin, after all. It won't hurt him any to add a few of *my* murders to his list."

"…………"

"You may think you're some sort of hero, but you were played like a puppet by a killer. How pathetic! Everything you tried to protect was an illusion. There is only one absolute in this world—fear."

Her voice grew stronger. Nagi's head was down. She wasn't moving, but she was whispering something.

"……………….not…"

Her voice was too soft to hear.

"Eh? What?" Makiko stepped closer.

"…not that I'm not scared. I'm just…"

She couldn't quite make it out. Makiko stepped even closer, her face right next to Nagi's. "What? I can't hear you."

"I'm just…worried."

"Worried? About what?"

"…that it'll fail."

Her voice was very weak.

"Fail? What will fail?"

"Well…this attack!" Nagi roared.

The arm she'd kept hidden in the muddy water thrust forward, clutching some sort of staff. It was one of the objects that had spilled out of her bag a moment before.

"_____!"

Makiko reacted quickly. The weapon darted past her chin, touching only air.

But she had not expected the attack, and it unbalanced her.

Nagi's movement did not stop there.

"......nargh!"

With a grunt, she stabbed the weapon into the water. It was a stun-rod that had been altered to remove all limitations, releasing extremely high-voltage electricity into the water where Nagi herself was sitting.

A horrendous electric current shot through Makiko's body. The water they were in was no ordinary water—Nagi had spilled her bag deliberately, filling the small pool with materials that conducted electricity well.

"......aughghghghghghghghgh!!"

Makiko arched backwards as electricity ran up her spine. A shock more powerful than anything else she had ever experienced ripped through her body.

While Nagi, on the other hand...there was smoke rising from her here and there, but she was standing upright, unaffected. She was wearing a custom-made insulated jumpsuit.

Of course, if the current had traveled up the water covering her body and reached her exposed head she would have died instantly. It had been quite a gamble.

"That's why I was worried," Nagi said, tossing aside the rod, which had shorted itself out. She pulled another one from her belt, extending it.

"Unghghghghghgh…!" the Fear Ghoul groaned, flinging herself at Nagi.

But a second later, Nagi's body moved like a piece of paper carried by the wind, and swept the Fear Ghoul's legs out from under her.

Nagi's hands only appeared to twist lightly. But with that, the overwhelmingly powerful monster spun in the air, crashing to the ground. The movement was less like karate and more like Aikido. It was almost a sort of sleight of hand. The monster's body slammed into the puddle, and then Nagi zapped it again.

"…………!!"

She screamed without making a sound.

It was clear which of them had won. Makiko could not understand what had happened.

How?

Why…?

Why, what, and how had things turned out like this...?

How can this be?!

Her entire body was numb, her limbs flailing wildly, her electrocuted body unable to move freely.

"Why?! How did...!"

Nagi grabbed her flailing arm, twisting it at the joint.

"...why...?!"

She tried to struggle anyway, and then it happened:

—Snap.

Like a dry twig breaking, the arm Nagi was holding tore right off.

"......?!"

The force Nagi had been using knocked her over. But Makiko showed no reaction to the loss of her arm, just crawling away on her remaining three limbs, trying to run, faster than any human could possibly move.

"W-wait!" Nagi yelped, jumping up. But her legs were still throbbing with pain, and she toppled over again.

As she tried to right herself once more, she heard a voice.

"I'm surprised," it said.

"......?!"

Nagi looked around. The person was close by.

"I did not expect you to escape that danger on your own. I took too long catching up with you, but it appears to have turned out well enough."

It was a strange voice, like a boy's, like a girl's, like both at once.

"Wh-who are you?!" Nagi called out. But the person did not answer.

"Leave the rest to me," it said, instead, and was gone.

Her entire body felt numb.

There was no pain from the ragged stump of her arm, just a vague sensation. She could no longer even remember who she was, as though her memories were covered in mist.

She had met something utterly terrifying. Something very frightening had happened to her. She remembered that much, if only because she was now running. Running away from it, yes, but away from *what*? Her confused mind could not remember. She felt like she had once had a grand purpose, but that purpose was now far, far away.

The powerful electric current had caused her evolving body to lose its balance. What had once been growing rapidly was now disintegrating at twice the speed, but she couldn't even tell what was happening.

For a moment, the waves had crested, but then they passed by, the current washing past her, into the distance—gone forever.

There were little popping noises all over her body as parts of it started breaking down.

Still, she did not stop. She *could not* stop. She was scared. Terrified. It felt like everything in the world was after her, and she was trembling violently, her teeth chattering.

"Eek! Eeeeeek…!"

Tears poured down her face. What had she done wrong? How had this happened to her?

"Eeeeeeeeeee…!"

She could only assume that *everything* had

been wrong. She felt that just being alive had been a mistake.

If she was going to be this scared, this frightened, then she was better off never having been born. Why was this happening to her? Why…?

She heard something in the distance. It was a strange sound—bright, yet somehow lonely. It was the sound of whistling carried on the wind. It was impossible to determine its source.

She looked up. She'd heard that music before.

"A proper fight to the death? Like a duel?"

Those words floated across her mind. Words she had said herself.

When had that been? Who had she been talking to? She couldn't remember, but she knew there was at least one reason why she could not afford to be afraid.

Yes.

Him.

He was here.

I have to fight with him. We promised. No remorse.

No time for fear. I have to face him down.

"…ah ha!"

The smile was back on her lips.

"Ah ha! Ah ha ha! Ah ha ha ha ha ha…!"

She stopped running, and turned around, facing down the entire world. "I'll take you on anytime! Come at me any way you like!"

Her voice was very feeble, barely able to claw its way out of her crumbling throat, but to her ears it sounded proud and haughty.

From behind her came the response, "I will."

Even as the voice spoke, there was the sound of something slicing through the air.

She tried to turn around, but she suddenly realized everything was already spinning.

The sky, the earth, her own body, everything around her—she could see her headless body crumpling to the ground. But if she could see that, then that meant…

Uhm…?

As the world spun, she saw a shadow flit across her field of vision. The shadow wore a strange, asymmetrical expression, like it was smiling. Like it was crying.

That was it. The microfilament wire snaked out at the speed of lightning, cutting Kisugi Makiko's head clean off. It spun through the air and fell to the ground.

5

When Nagi returned, Mo Murder was on the brink of death. His wound was mortal, but he had lived for several minutes despite that—a testament to the strength he had been given. Like Makiko said, he was not human. Despite his inhuman power, there was no saving him now.

"…Sasaki-san," Nagi said. "Any last words?"

Breathing raggedly, Mo Murder tried to speak. Nagi leaned closer.

"…I'm glad…you survived," he said. "The bug…isn't that bad…"

That was all.

"…………"

Nagi stood up.

"The bug…?" she said, reflectively.

She looked behind her. A strange figure in a black hat and cloak stood there. It was the one who had spoken to her earlier.

"What do you think that means?"

"No idea. But if he says it isn't bad, then that's all you need to know. He seems to have been satisfied just knowing you're alive. Isn't that enough?"

Nagi couldn't tell if the figure was a boy or a girl. He seemed about Nagi's age, but she couldn't be sure. There was white makeup and black lipstick on his face.

"I suppose…but…what are you? You followed me all the way here, but why did you finish off Kisugi Makiko?"

"You were the one that defeated her."

"…I'm not so sure," Nagi said, scowling. "I feel like this whole affair was a trainwreck. Not one thing went right…"

"Not everything does," the cloaked figure said, oddly confident. It was a strange way of speaking—expressing conviction without reason.

"What do they call you?"

"You mean my name?"

"…what else would I mean?"

"Fair enough," the cloaked figure said, thinking about it. Then he nodded. "I shall call myself Boogiepop."

"…that's a weird name."

"You could say that as well, Kirima Nagi."

Nagi nodded, ruefully.

She turned serious again. "…what should we do about…the leftovers?"

"Forget them. Someone else will clean up," Boogiepop said, disinterested.

Nagi glared at him, but he just shrugged.

"There are forces at work behind this. Major ones. Leaving things to them will cause less trouble," he said, calmly.

That did seem to be true, Nagi thought. "So Sasaki-san will be the killer?"

"If the world knew a doctor was behind it, there would be panic. All the patients she treated would be looked at with suspicion. And I doubt "Sasaki-san" would want that. He would have been happy to take the blame. Anything for you."

"…………"

Nagi did not look satisfied.

"What went wrong?" she muttered. What terrible thing had happened that brought all this to pass?

"Must be the bug," Boogiepop said.

Nagi looked up.

"The world is not moving unrelentingly in one direction. It moves in all directions, like a swarm of bugs. Sometimes they make one unified motion, but other times, like this case, the movement simply collapses, without ever resulting in anything. That is all."

"Then what should I do?" Nagi asked, her voice tight. "How can I stop this from happening again? What can I do to make things turn out better?"

Boogiepop frowned. "You intend to try again?"

Nagi glared at him. "Is that a problem?"

"No…but if that's the case, then this is not goodbye."

"Eh?"

"We may well meet again, many times, in similar circumstances," he said, with a wink.

"I suppose." Nagi shook her head.

When she looked up again, the cloaked figure was gone. He had vanished in an instant.

"…………"

She stood stunned for a moment, but then shook her head again, "Oh well," she said.

Then she slowly walked away, dragging her injured leg. She glanced back at the body once, but soon moved forward again. This time she did not stop.

The full moon above bathed the world in its constant glow.

"The Bug" closed.

CHAPTER 7
The Piper at the Gates of Dawn "Reprise"

"That's all."

In the world covered in ruins, everything crumbled and destroyed, Boogiepop's story ended.

"I see," Echoes said, nodding gravely. "Nothing can be explained easily. Everything is complicated…"

He sighed.

Boogiepop silently nodded in assent.

It was dawn now. The sky was turning pale.

The air never moved. If either of them dropped something, it would undoubtedly echo without end.

Boogiepop began to whistle, and Echoes began to hum along. He had only heard it once, but he remembered the melody.

For a while, they performed in chorus. No one

else was here to listen, and the melody drifted around them quietly.

As they did, the world began to change.

The horizons grew indistinct, like an out of focus camera. The blur was drawing closer to them, but their performance continued.

Eventually the world was only in focus for a few meters around them, and only then did their song end.

"…I've never sung before," Echoes said, grinning. "It was very enjoyable."

Boogiepop again produced that asymmetrical expression, half smile, half smirk.

"This world is almost finished. We must say good-bye, Echoes-kun, but I'm glad we met."

"Yes. I am grateful that we were brought together here. I know not what quirk of fate it was, but just as Kirima Nagi carries on her fight, accepting the feelings of those she meets, I am grateful for what fate has done. Thank you," he said quietly, placing his hand on his chest.

Boogiepop nodded lightly.

The world around them was vanishing quickly.

"Where will you go now?" Boogiepop asked.

Echoes smiled. "I will watch over the world from a distance. No matter what happens to me. Yes…I'm just taking my turn."

"I see."

"And you? Boogiepop, what will you do?"

"Well…" he shrugged. "First off, I'd better meet the Piper—he made this world before Zoragi destroyed it. He appears to be waiting for me."

His eyes looked rather stern.

"And then? You will fight on?"

"Well…" Boogiepop started to answer, but the vanishing of the world had reached Echoes.

His figure went out of synch with this world, blurred, and was gone.

All that remained was Boogiepop.

"…so," he said, absently.

And, left all alone, he began to whistle once more.

"_____♪"

Even time had vanished. Only the hazy light of dawn remained. And there, Boogiepop whistled quietly, his whistle reaching nowhere, and no one.

"Boogiepop at Dawn" all over.

AFTERWORD
Beginnings

Erm. Most of the time, when people are ready to start something, they have already stuck their noses in pretty far. Take the phenomenon known as love at first sight; it does not actually begin at the chance meeting. First, that person's heart has to be ready for such an encounter. That way, when he runs across someone who perfectly fits that form, he falls in love. This readiness is not always based on an ideal type, but can also be based purely on negative emotions, whittled down by his reactions to things he hates until a form is made unconsciously. When something appears that is the inverse of these negative emotions, the person falls as though the ground underfoot has crumbled. Thus, nothing in the world ever truly begins; there is always a certain amount of preparation beforehand.

To give an example, this happened when I was still a student. I was staring vacantly at the street below out the window of a train stopped at JR Yuraku-cho Station when I thought I saw a black shadow in the middle of the crowd. I'm nearsighted, and I soon lost track of whatever it was…I think. I was pretty out of it, so it might just have been my imagination. I spent most of my time rather dazed back then. But this thing was like a black mass rising directly out of the ground, like a *youkai* or spirit. Perhaps I never really saw it, but just thought something like that might be neat.

At the time, I was already writing novels (during class…so consistently that even people I didn't know knew that I was writing novels…incorrigible) so you might say I should have just written about that, but at the time I was writing a different kind of novel and didn't feel like it. My head was full of that one thing, and I never even looked at anything else; but looking back at it, even then I was interested in all kinds of things, and I did spend a lot of my time on unrelated matters. I had started listening to music, but I had no intention of connecting that interest to my writing. It was just for fun. That's still partly true, even now. I did several other things that had equally little effect on my writing. They should have had everything to do with it, but I never noticed. And the shadow I saw out the window of the train was just one tiny piece of this.

So when I did decide to write about it, all the preparations that I needed to write about it had already been done. I don't really know how. When I started I was all revved up to begin and I poured my energy into it. Yet, apparently, it had already started long before. Apparently everything works that way. Even if you fail constantly, if you end up slamming your face into the wall over and over, you are already starting something, and no matter how fruitless and depressing it might seem to be, even if it really *is* sad, nothing can stop it from starting. Even if nothing lies ahead of you but darkness.

I think.

This looks optimistic, but it really isn't.
Oh well.

BGM "The Beginning is the End is the Beginning"
by THE SMASHING PUMPKINS

TRANSLATION NOTES

The End is the Beginning is the End

Nagi's name
凪 means "calm" in the sense of a lack of wind. It clearly contains the same metaphorical connotations in both languages; the kanji looks a little like 風—*kaze* or "wind."

Style

Flock of Crows
Technically a "murder of crows," but in this context that was confusing.

Public Enemy No. 1

Love & Revolution
"Man was born for love and revolution," are the words of author Osamu Dazai. They come from his novel *Shayo, The Setting Sun*.

Green
Mijukumono, an inexperienced person. Literally means "Unripened."

Child is the Father to the Man
In keeping with Kadono's tradition of musical references, an album title by Blood, Sweat & Tears. A discovery made because that was how I was able to trace it back to the English expression…

A Three Year Old's Soul Lasts a Hundred Years
The Japanese expression "*Mitsugo no tamashii hyaku made*—translated fairly literally, but with an eye on preserving the actual meaning. Another translation is, "What is learned in the cradle is carried to the grave."

The Piper at the Gates
of Dawn "Reprise"

I'm Just Taking My Turn
"Ano hito no kawari ni" is literally, "In place of that person." It is unclear who Echoes is talking about.

Piper
Waikyokuou is translated literally as "The King of Distortion," but it appears to be a quotation from the Japanese translation of the lyrics to *Stairway to Heaven*. Apparently that's how some poetic translator chose to render "Piper." The character of Piper plays a role in the fifth *Boogiepop* novel entitled *Boogiepop Overdrive*.

Zoragi
Zoragi is a rubber suit style monster that also appears in the fifth novel.

KOUHEI KADONO

A frustrated man wandering through life. He moves at one speed, and he was left behind before he realized it. Wrote a novel about a hitman when he was nineteen that, in retrospect, may have been of critical importance. It also might just have been a sign that he hasn't progressed at all.

KOUJI OGATA

Born in 1970. Osaka Resident. Barely managed to get enough credits to graduate from Osaka Design School. Did a lot of things after that, which brings us to the present. Enjoys motorcycles, tennis, and remote controlled models. Popular and frantically busy. Likes to drink.